Joan C Baez

and then I wrote . . .

This volume contains all of the compositions written by Joan to date. Compositions by others and recorded by Joan will appear in "AND THEN I SANG . . .," to be published in the near future.

Original Line Drawings by JOAN BAEZ
Design Concept by JOAN BAEZ and NANCY CARLEN
Production Work by NANCY CARLEN and RUTH VALPEY
Cover Photo & Pages 114-115 ⓒ JIM MARSHALL

THIS BOOK IS DEDICATED TO ALLEN WHEELIS

Drawings and Poetry

See page 116 for Music Section

Gossamer

Lyrics by Nina Duscheck
Music by Joan Baez

When I was young then all my boughs
were thickly hung with glittering hopes.
But one by one they've blown away
and only one remains today.
It flutters out upon the air,
one hope all pinned on gossamer.

What are all lives but gossamer
in one lacy cobweb crossed?
Yet strand by strand we tear at it
until the pattern's lost.
And one by one hopes blow away
till only one remains today.

I hope the forest will return
to climb the mist-hung morning slopes.
Where falling leaves deep-banked in fern
may meet the water ouzel's hopes.
'But one by one they've blown away
and only one remains today.

And when the condor opens flight
on crystal air not cracked or stained
by any fallen angel's flight,
these glittering hopes may be regained.

When I was young then all my boughs
were thickly hung with glittering hopes.
But one by one they've blown away
and only one remains today.
It flutters out upon the air,
one hope all pinned on gossamer.

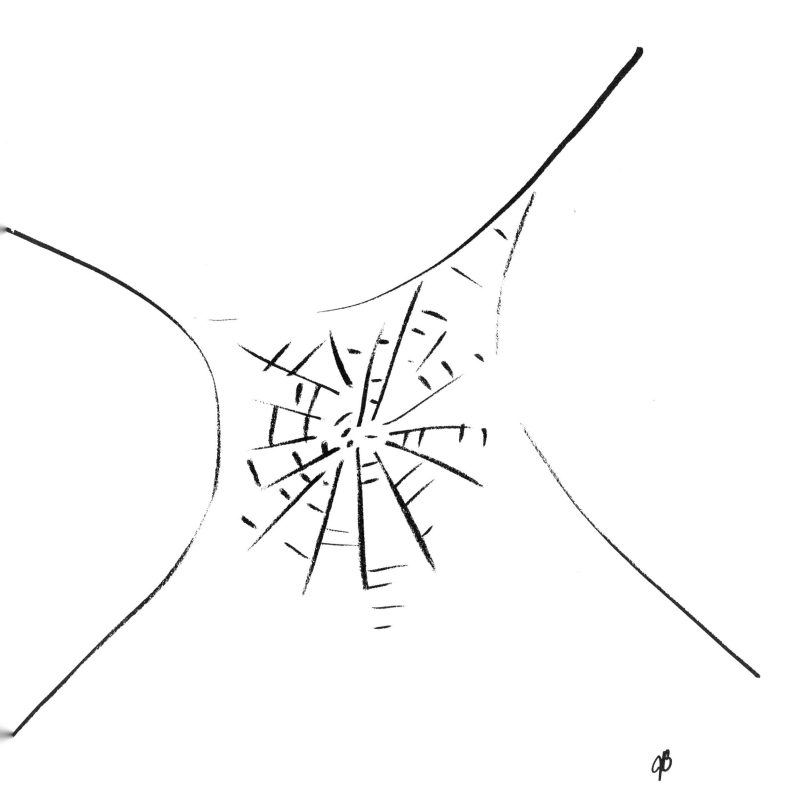

Saigon Bride

Lyrics by Nina Duscheck
Music by Joan Baez

Farewell my wistful Saigon bride,
I'm going out to stem the tide.
A tide that never saw the seas,
it flows through jungles, round the trees.
Some say it's yellow, some say red,
it will not matter when we're dead.

How many dead men will it take
to build a dike that will not break?
How many children must we kill
before we make the waves stand still?

Though miracles come high today,
we have the wherewithal to pay.
It takes them off the streets you know,
to places they would never go alone.
It gives them useful trades.
The lucky boys are even paid.

Men die to build their Pharaoh's tombs,
and still and still the teeming wombs.
How many men to conquer Mars,
how many dead to reach the stars?

Farewell my wistful Saigon bride,
I'm going out to stem the tide.
A tide that never saw the seas,
it flows through jungles, round the trees.
Some say it's yellow, some say red,
it will not matter when we're dead.

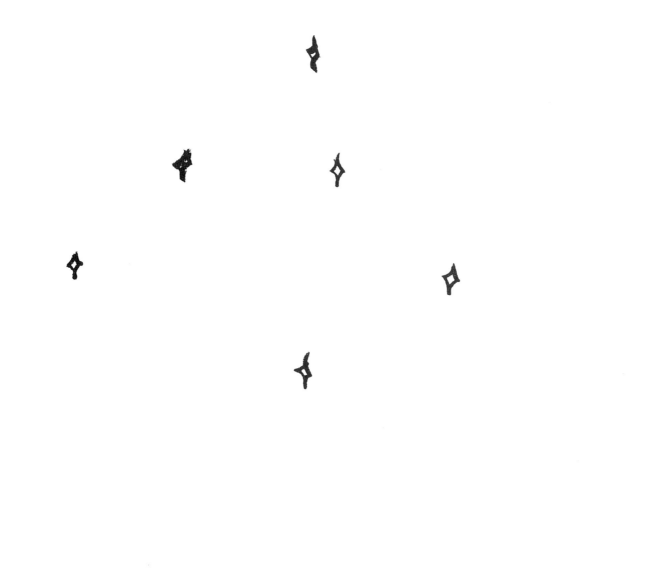

North

Lyrics by Nina Duscheck
Music by Joan Baez

Where icicles hung the blossoms swing,
but in my heart there is no spring.
You were my spring, my summer too,
it's always winter without you.

The flocks head north and the lilacs bloom,
at night they scent my moonlit room.
You were my spring, my summer too,
I'm going north to look for you.

Like a windblown bird my heart goes forth,
sent by the spring to the shining north.
You are my spring, my summer too,
and I won't rest till I find you.

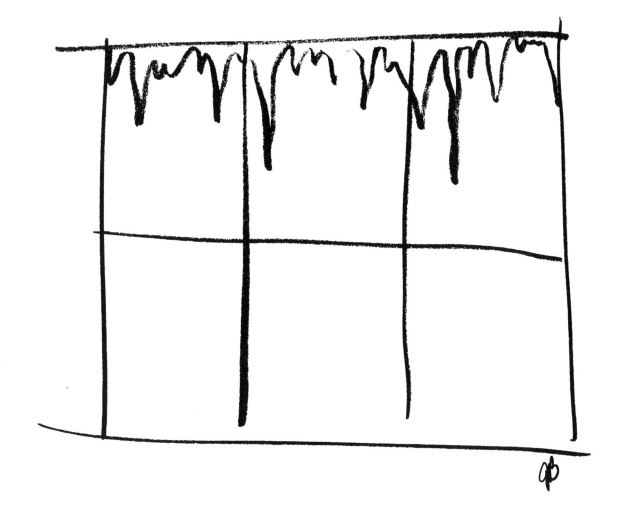

Sweet Sir Galahad

Words and Music by Joan Baez

Sweet Sir Galahad
came in through the window
in the night when
the moon was in the yard.
He took her hand in his
and shook the long hair
from his neck and he told her
she'd been working much too hard.
It was true that ever since the day
her crazy man had passed away
to the land of poet's pride,
she laughed and talked a lot
with new people on the block
but always at evening time she cried.

And here's to the dawn
of their days.

She moved her head
a little down on the bed
until it rested softly on his knee.
And there she dropped her smile
and there she sighed awhile,
and told him all the sadness
of those years that numbered three.
Well you know I think my fate's belated
because of all the hours I waited
for the day when I'd no longer cry.
I get myself to work by eight
but oh was I born too late
and do you think I'll fail
at every single thing I try?

And here's to the dawn
of their days.

He just put his arm around her
and that's the way I found her
eight months later to the day.
The lines of a smile erased
the tear tracks upon her face,
a smile that could linger even stay.
Sweet Sir Galahad went down
with his gay bride of flowers,
the prince of the hours
of her lifetime.

And here's to the dawn
of their days,
of their days.

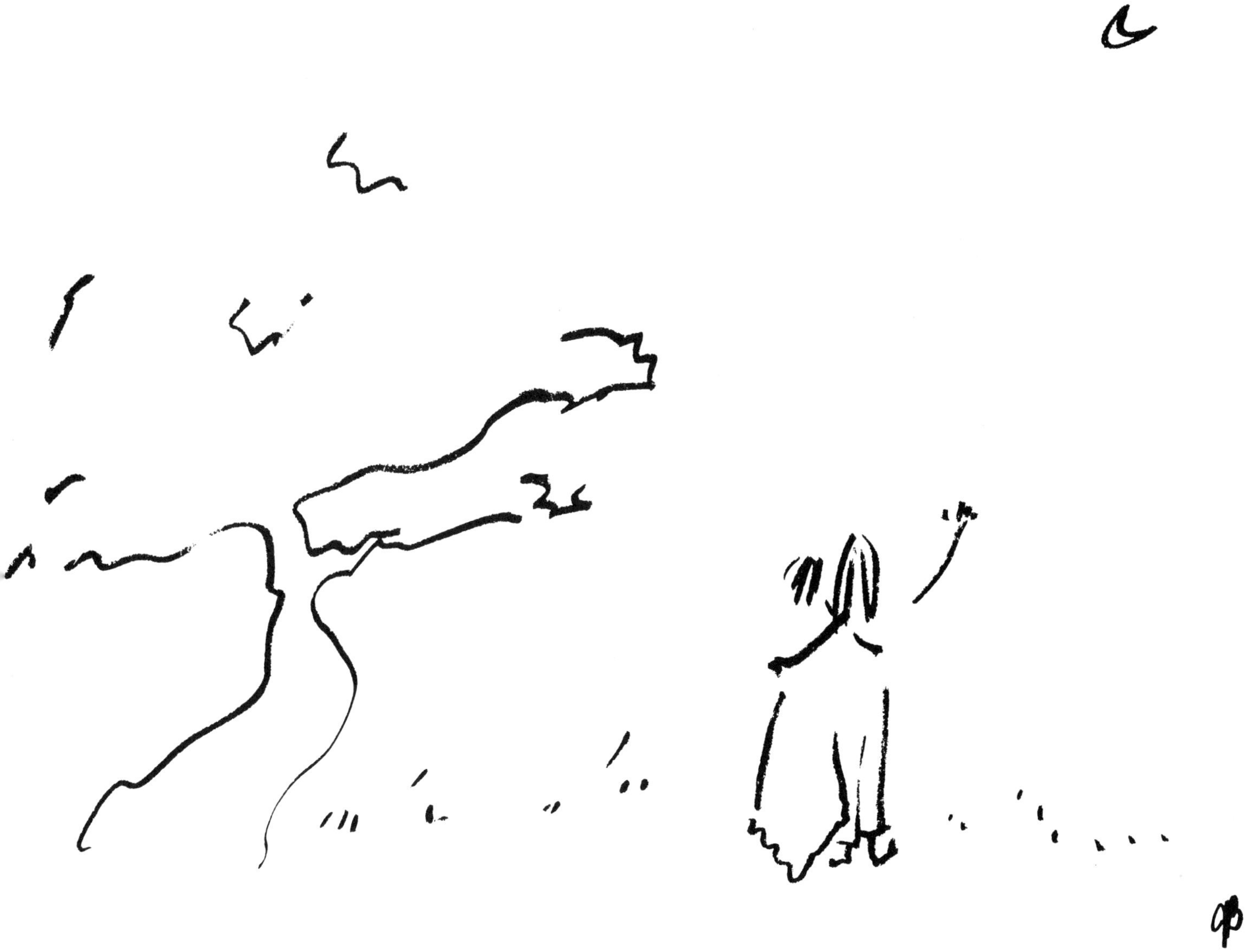

A Song For David

Words and Music by Joan Baez

In my heart I will wait
by the stony gate
and the little one
in my arms will sleep.
Every rising of the moon
makes the years grow late
and the love in our hearts will keep.
There are friends I will make
and bonds I will break
as the seasons roll by
and we build our own sky.
In my heart I will wait
by the stony gate
and the little one
in my arms will sleep.

And the stars in your sky
are the stars in mine
and both prisoners
of this life are we.
Through the same troubled waters
we carry our time,
you and the convicts and me.
There's a good thing to know,
on the outside or in,
to answer not where
but just who I am.
Because the stars in your sky
are the stars in mine
and both prisoners
of this life are we.

And the hills that you know
will remain for you
and the little willow green
will stand firm.
The flowers that we planted
through the seasons past
will all bloom
on the day you return.
To a baby at play
all a mother can say,
he'll return on the wind
to our hearts, and till then,
I will sit and I'll wait
by the stony gate,
and the little one
'neath the trees will dance.

Blessed Are

Words and Music by Joan Baez

'Blessed are the one-way ticket holders
on a one-way street.
'Blessed are the midnight riders
for in the shadow of God they sleep.
'Blessed are the huddled hikers
staring out at falling rain,
wondering at the retribution
in their personal acquaintance with pain.
'Blessed are the blood relations
of the young ones who have died,
who had not the time or patience
to carry on this earthly ride.
'Rain will come and winds will blow,
wild deer die in the mountain snow.
'Birds will beat at heaven's wall,
what comes to one must come to us all.

'For you and I are one-way ticket holders
on a one-way street,
which lies across a golden valley
where the waters of joy and hope run deep.
So if you pass the parents weeping
of the young ones who have died,
take them to your warmth and keeping
for blessed are the tears they cried
and many were the years they tried.
'Take them to that valley wide
and let their souls be pacified.

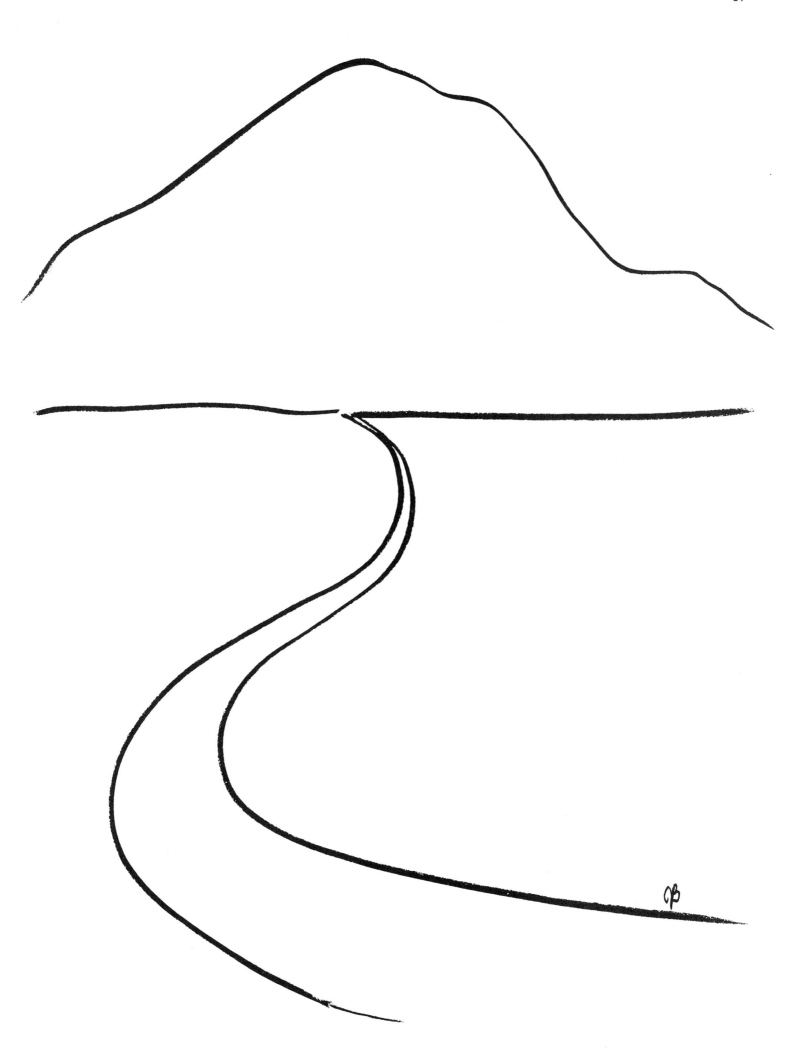

Three Horses

Words and Music by Joan Baez

In the early dawn a stallion white
prances the hills in the morning light.
His bridle is painted with thunder and gold,
orchids and dragons, pale knights of old.
He is the horse of the ages past.
And now the children run to see
the stallion on the hill,
bringing bags of apples
and of clover they have filled.
And the white horse tells his stories
of the days now past and gone
and the children stand a-wondering
believing every song.
How brightly glows the past.

When the sun is high comes a mare so red,
trampling the graves of the living and dead.
Her mantle is heavy with mirrors and glass,
all is reflected when the red mare does pass.
She is the horse of the here and now.
And now there is confusion
amongst the children on the hill.
They cling to one another
and no longer can be still.
While the red mare's voice is trembling
with a rare and mighty call,
the children start remembering
the bearers and the pall.
and though their many-colored sweaters
are reflected in the glass,
and though the sun shines down upon them,
they are frightened in the grass.
How stark is the here and now.

When night does fall comes a stallion black,
so proud and tall he never looks back.
He wears him no emeralds, silver and gold,
not even a covering to keep him from cold.
He is the horse of the years to come.
And I will get me down
before this steed upon my knees
and sing to him the sorrows
of a thousand centuries.
And the children now will scatter
as their mothers call them home,
for the sadness of the evening horse
no child has ever known.
And I will hang about him
a bell that's never rung
and thank him for the many words
which from his throat have never sprung.
And I'll thank God and all the angels
that the stallion of the evening,
the black horse of the future,
comes to earth but has no tongue.

Last, Lonely And Wretched

Words and Music by Joan Baez

You're tired and you're poor,
you long to be free,
but in this Godforsaken land
you find no home, no family
on the many roads that you've wandered
since the day of your birth.
You've become one of the last,
lonely and wretched.

Your hair is matted,
your face and hands are dirty,
and the years that you've toiled
must number somewhere near thirty.
The deepening of a sadness
broke finally into madness.
You are truly one of the
last, lonely and wretched.

Your eyes are wild and frightening
at the same time they are blessed
and I wonder if God died,
turned his back or only just rested.
And you walked out on the seventh day
through the big gates and on your way
to become one of the
last, lonely and wretched.

For once you were a child.
Your cheeks were red,
you were well fed.
You laughed and played
till you got teary,
ran to your mother
when you were weary.

But somewhere you were forsaken
alone I'll not bear the blame
and somehow all was taken,
your mind, your body, your name.
Forgive us our unkindness,
our desertion and our blindness,
with you, all the last,
lonely and wretched.
Forgive us, all the
last, lonely and wretched.

Outside The Nashville City Limits

Words and Music by Joan Baez

Outside the Nashville city limits
a friend and I did drive,
on a day in early winter
I was glad to be alive.
We went to see some friends of his
who lived upon a farm.
Strange and gentle country folk
who would wish nobody harm.
Fresh-cut sixty acres,
eight cows in the barn.
But the thing that I remember
on that cold day in December
was that my eyes they did brim over
as we talked.

In the slowest drawl
I had ever heard
the man said "Come with me
if y'all wanna see the prettiest place
in all of Tennessee."
He poured us each a glass of wine
and a-walking we did go,
along fallen leaves and crackling ice
where a tiny brook did flow.
He knew every inch of the land
and Lord he loved it so.
But the thing that I remember
on that cold day in December
was that my eyes were brimming over
as we walked.

He set me down upon a stone
beside a running spring.
He talked in a voice
so soft and clear,
like the waters I heard sing.
He said "We searched quite a time
for a place to call our own.
There was just me and Mary John,
and now I guess we're home."
I looked at the ground and wondered
how many years they each had roamed.
And Lord I do remember
on that day in late December
how my eyes kept brimming over
as we talked.
As we walked.

And standing there
with outstretched arms
he said to me "You know,
I can't wait until the heavy storms
cover the ground with snow,
and there on the pond the watercress
is all that don't turn white.
When the sun is high you squint your eyes
and look at the hills so bright."
And nodding his head my friend said,
"And it seems like overnight
that the leaves come out so tender
at the turning of the winter . . ."
I thought the skies they would brim over
as we talked.

When Time Is Stolen

Words and Music by Joan Baez

The music stopped in my hand,
my hand,
my hand.
Sadly smiled the band,
the band,
the band.
Softly echoes your laughter,
riddled with tears.
When time is stolen it flies,
it flies,
it flies.
Lovers leave in disguise,
disguise,
disguise.
Weariness hangs like a curtain,
heavy and old,
heavy and cold.

It is said to never look back,
look back,
look back.
To shadows you left on the track,
the track,
the track.
Gather your roses
and run the long way around.
And if time should ever be right,
my love,
my love,
I'll come to you in the night,
my love,
my love.
But now there is only the sorrow,
parting is near,
parting is here.
Parting is here,
parting is here.

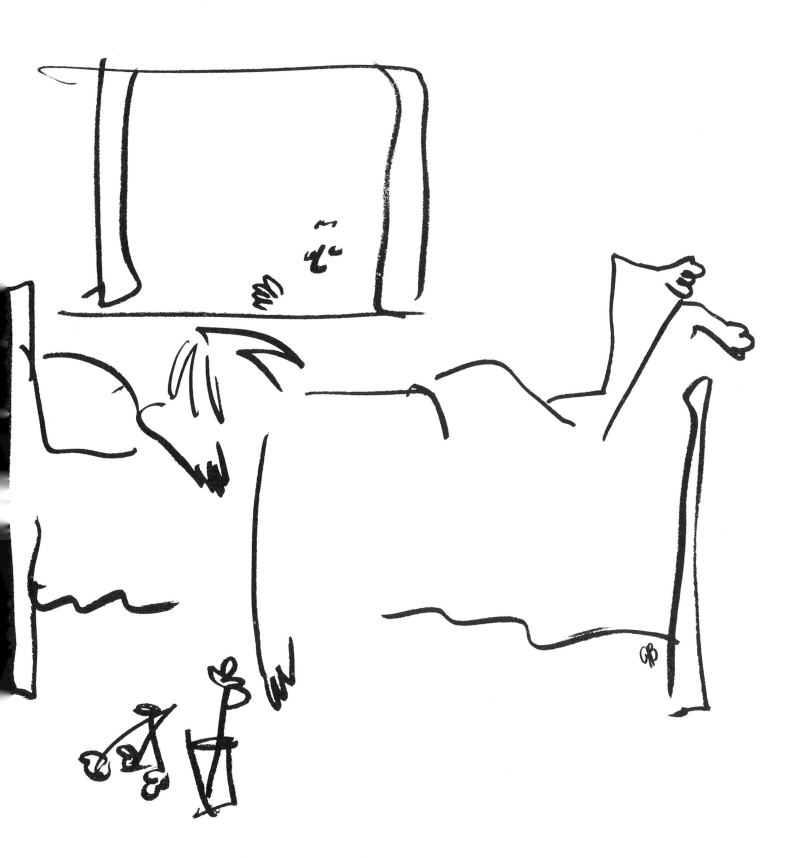

Gabriel And Me

Words and Music by Joan Baez

The grey quiet horse
wears the reins of dawn,
and nobody knows
what mountain he's from.
In his mouth he carries
the golden key,
and nobody sees him
but Gabriel and me.
Gabriel and me.

His nose is silver
and his mane is white.
His eyes are black
and starry like night.
So softly he splashes
his hooves in the sea
that nobody hears him
but Gabriel and me.
Gabriel and me.

He comes in the morning
when the air is still.
He races the sun
and he always will.
We raise up the window
and call through the trees,
oh we'd love to fly with you,
Gabriel and me.
Gabriel and me.

For your back is wingless
and there's room for two.
We'll mount from a tree
and ride straight on through.
But I guess you're wiser
than I thought you'd be,
for you never will listen
to Gabriel and me.
Gabriel and me.

For you know that one day
we'll forget to wake.
Call it destiny,
call it fate.
You'll nuzzle us softly,
and so silently
we'll ride in the morning,
Gabriel and me,
with the golden key.
Gabriel and me,
forever to the sea.

Milanese Waltz
Instrumental

Marie Flore
Words and Music by Joan Baez

Marie, Marie Flore,
was a small girl of ten
whom I met
in the south end of France.
Stepping out of a crowd
was the daughter of someone
with flowers for me;
we were friends at a glance.
She spoke no English
but sat by my side in the car,
pointing out places
en route to the village of Arles.

Marie, Marie Flore,
came to table that night
as I dined in an ancient hotel.
The room was all fitted
with things from the seventeenth century
and they suited her well.
She would eat nothing
but sat in her chair like a queen;
and laughed at my French,
but seemed always to know what I'd mean.

Marie, Marie Flore,
came to hear me that night
when I sang for the people of Arles.
She stood back in the shadows
of a ruined arena;
her frame in my mind was never too far.
In the rush that did follow
I found she was holding my hand;
and ushering me through an evening
the elders had planned.

Marie, Marie Flore,
I will always remember
your eyes, your smile and your grace.
The gold that flowed with your laughter
remains to enlighten the image
I have of your face.
For I have seen children
with faces much wiser than time;
and you, my Marie,
are most certainly one of this kind.

Marie, Marie Flore,
all the odds say I'll see you again
by plan or by chance.
But if not you'll be there
when I'm dreaming of rain over Paris
or sun on the south end of France.
Marie, Marie, Marie Flore.

The Hitchhikers' Song

Words and Music by Joan Baez

When the mist rolls in
on Highway One
like a curtain to the day,
a thousand silhouettes
hold out their thumbs.
And I see them and I say,
you are my children,
my sweet children.
I am your poet.
With hair just like
the burning tree of Moses,
the girl beside you
is your twin.
And beneath your fiery make-up
you should know this,
I am your sister,
I am your kin.
Your flesh and kin.
I'll write this tune
in matching phrases
just to show it.

You are the orphans
in an age of no tomorrows.
And with your walking
you wage a war
against the sorrows.
Your fathers left you
a road to hoe,
and you'll hoe it.
If I could write you
easy directions on a list
you would not read it,
you could not see it,
for the mist.
Besides, my pen is very righteous
and I know it.

So walk to the edges
of a dying kingdom.
There's one more summer
just around the bend.
The amber in your smile
is brave and winsome,
for though your highway has no end,
it never ends.
There is still the sky,
the windy cliff,
and the sea below it.
I'd take an angel's
ram's horn trumpet
and I'd blow it,
I'd blow it.

Fifteen Months

Words and Music by Joan Baez

The cats are sleeping
here in the autumn sun.
Your dog has flushed a deer
and he's on the run.
And the coffee cup is cold,
and the morning's feeling very old.

Fifteen months of time
my man's been gone.
The second winter
now is coming on.
And our fates could all be worse.
But sometimes I still must curse my own.

And hello, I wish you well
where you sleep all in your cell.

As for friends,
I can't complain,
they've been good to me.
The fire's burning bright,
they've left wood for me.
And the roof has been repaired.
And I thank them for the love they've shared.

You see, there's really nothing wrong,
I've just got the blues.
Because if you give a damn,
you're going to pay some dues.
But if you see the game we're in,
like I do, you know in time we'll win.

And hello, I wish you well
where you sleep all in your cell.

So time give me a break
of a week or more.
My head is reeling
and my back is sore.
And the baby cries for me.
And I think I'll walk by the sea alone.

Prison Trilogy

Words and Music by Joan Baez

Billy Rose was a low rider,
Billy Rose was a night fighter,
Billy Rose knew trouble
like the sound of his own name.
Busted on a drunken charge
driving someone else's car,
the local midnight sheriff's
claim to fame.
In an Arizona jail
there are some who tell the tale
how Billy fought the sergeant
for some milk that he demanded,
knowing they'd remain the boss,
knowing he would pay the cost.
They saw he was severely reprimanded.
In the blackest cell on A Block
he hanged himself at dawn.
With a note stuck to the bunkhead,
"Don't mess with me,
just take me home."

    Come and lay,
    help us lay
    poor Billy down.

Luna was a Mexican
the law called an alien
for coming 'cross the border
with a baby and a wife.
While the clothes upon his back were wet,
still he thought that he could get
some money and the things to start a life.
It hadn't been too very long
when it seemed like everything went wrong.
Didn't even have the time
to find themselves a home
when this foreigner,
a brown skinned male
thrown inside a Texas jail,
left his wife and baby quite alone.
He eased the pain inside him
with a needle in his arm,
but the dope just crucified him
and he died to no one's great alarm.

    Come and lay,
    help us lay
    poor Luna down.

    And we'll raze,
    raze the prisons
    to the ground.

Kilowatt was an aging con of sixty-five
who stood a chance to stay alive
and leave the joint
and walk the streets again.
As the time he was to leave drew near,
he suffered all the joy and fear
of leaving thirty-five years in the pen.
Then on the day of his release
he was approached by the police
who took him to the warden
walking slowly by his side.
The warden said you won't remain here
but it seems a state retainer
claims another ten years of your life.
He stepped out in the Texas sunlight
and the cops all stood around.
Old Kilowatt ran fifty yards
then threw himself down on the ground.
They might as well
just have laid that old man down.

    But we're going to raze,
    raze the prisons
    to the ground.

    Help us raze,
    raze the prisons
    to the ground.

38

Love Song To A Stranger

Words and Music by Joan Baez

How long since I've spent a whole night
in a twin bed with a stranger,
his warm arms all around me?
How long since I've gazed into dark eyes
that melted my soul down
to a place where it longs to be?
All of your history
has little to do with your face.
You're mainly a mystery
with violins filling in space.

You stood in the nude by the mirror
and picked out a rose
from the bouquet in our hotel,
and lay down beside me again.
And I watched the rose
on the pillow where it fell.
I sank and I slept in a twilight
with only one care,
to know that when day broke
and I woke that you'd still be there.

The hours for once
they passed slowly, unendingly by,
like a sweet breeze on a field.
Your gentleness came down upon me
and I guess I thanked you
when you caused me to yield.
We spoke not a sentence
and took not a footstep beyond
our two days together
which seemingly soon would be gone.

Don't tell me of love everlasting
and other sad dreams,
I don't want to hear.
Just tell me of passionate strangers
who rescue each other
from a lifetime of cares.
Because if love means forever
expecting nothing returned,
then I hope I'll be given
another whole lifetime to learn.

Because you gave to me
oh so many things,
it makes me wonder
how they could belong to me.
And I gave you only my dark eyes
that melted your soul down
to a place where it longs to be.

Copyright © 1972 Chandos Music

Love Song To A Stranger, Part II

Words and Music by Joan Baez

They brought me a beautiful basket of fruit
and two finger bowls of glass.
The couch is gold, with a floral design,
and the wine is Germany's best.
And the wine is Germany's best.

My thoughts drift into the frozen night,
Frankfurt is covered with snow,
and numbly they ride on an icy wind
to places they're longing to go.
To places they're longing to go.

I remember the tall dark Irish rose
who held me in my limousine,
and slept with me under a burgundy quilt
with sheets of silk in between.
Well, anyway, that's how it seemed.

I thought I wanted to marry him,
his face was sculpted by God.
His words were gentle and ever so true,
and soft as the Irish fog.
And lost in the Irish fog.

I remember the boy from the monastery,
who wanted to be a monk.
But he brought flowers and wine to my room,
and we both got happily drunk.
And we both got perfectly drunk.

He laughed like the chimes of a silver bell,
his eyes were alexandrite blue.
He danced the T'ai Chi with the grace of a deer
and I wanted to marry him too.
Yes I wanted to marry him too.

There was that son of a dog
from the Tennessee hills,
kept telling me I was still young.
He spoke in pure southern
and smoothed out the lines
round my eyes saying I was the one.
Forever that I'd be the one.

He drank and he cussed
and he wrote his own songs,
he was very much on the go.
We followed each other for over a year,
I couldn't have married him though.
So we just lived in sin on the road.

There was that black eyed beauty
from Boston town,
two days were never too long.
He stood by the mirror
and picked out a rose,
but I already wrote him a song.
Yes I already wrote him a song.

So here I sit with my basket of fruit,
and two finger bowls of glass.
I finished my bottle of Germany's best
and concluded my thoughts on the past,
that love is a pain in the ass.

42

Myths

Words and Music by Joan Baez

A myth has just been shattered,
upon the four winds scattered,
back to some storybook
from whence it came.
Vicarious hearts may ache,
and try to mend the break,
and seek for a righteous place
to put the blame.

Neither of us knew
what the future would bring.
We only know that now there is
some room to talk and sing.
The baby laughs a lot
and that's the most important thing.
And as soon as we can handle
the hurt and pain,
there may be more
than just happy memories to gain.

So to hell with all the troubles
and counting up the couples
who travelled this same route
on their way down.
Because if we keep on growing
there is no way of knowing
when we'll meet
as two new people we just found.
We just found.

All The Weary Mothers Of The Earth (People's Union #1)

Words and Music by Joan Baez

All the weary mothers
of the earth will finally rest.
We will take their babies
in our arms and do our best.
When the sun is low upon the field
to love and music they will yield.
And the weary mothers
of the earth shall rest.

And the farmer on his tractor
and beside his plow,
will stand there in confusion
as we wet his brow
with the tears of all the businessmen
who see what they have done to him.
And the weary farmers
of the earth shall rest.

And the aching workers
of the world again shall sing,
these words in mighty choruses
to all will bring:
"We shall no longer be the poor
for no one owns us anymore."
And the workers of the world
again shall sing.

And when the soldiers burn
their uniforms in every land,
the foxholes at the borders
will be left unmanned.
General, when you come for the review
the troops will have forgotten you.
And the men and women
of the earth shall rest.

To Bobby

Words and Music by Joan Baez

I'll put flowers at your feet
and I will sing to you so sweet,
and hope my words
will carry home to your heart.
You left us marching on the road,
and said how heavy was the load;
the years were young,
the struggle barely had its start.
Do you hear the voices in the night, Bobby?
They're crying for you.
See the children in the morning light, Bobby.
They're dying.

No one could say it like you said it;
we'd only try, and just forget it.
You stood alone upon the mountain
till it was sinking.
And in a frenzy
we tried to reach you,
with looks and letters
we would beseech you,
never knowing what, where,
or how you were thinking.
Do you hear the voices in the night, Bobby?
They're crying for you.
See the children in the morning light, Bobby.
They're dying.

Perhaps the pictures in the Times
can no longer be put in rhymes,
when all the eyes
of starving children are wide open.
You cast aside the cursed crown,
and put your magic into a sound
that made me think your heart
was aching, or even broken.
But if God hears my complaint
He will forgive you.
And so will I.
With all respect, I'll just re-live you.
And likewise, you must understand
these things we give you.

Like these flowers at your door,
and scribbled notes about the war.
We're only saying the time is short
and there is work to do.
And we're still marching in the streets,
with little victories and big defeats,
but there is joy and there is hope,
and there's a place for you.
And you have heard the voices in the night, Bobby.
They're crying for you.
See the children in the morning light, Bobby.
They're dying.

Song Of Bangladesh

Words and Music by Joan Baez

Bangladesh, Bangladesh.
Bangladesh, Bangladesh.
When the sun sinks in the west
die a million people
of the Bangladesh.

The story of Bangladesh
is an ancient one again made fresh
by blind men who carry out commands
which flow out of laws
upon which nations stand,
which say to sacrifice
a people for a land.

Bangladesh, Bangladesh.
Bangladesh, Bangladesh.
When the sun sinks in the west
die a million people
of the Bangladesh.

Once again we stand aside
and watch the families crucified.
See a teenage mother's vacant eyes
as she watches her feeble baby try
to fight the monsoon rains
and the cholera flies.

And the students at the university
asleep at night quite peacefully.
The soldiers came and shot them in their beds.
And terror took the dorm,
awakening shrieks of dread,
and silent frozen forms
and pillows drenched in red.

Bangladesh, Bangladesh.
Bangladesh, Bangladesh.
When the sun sinks in the west
die a million people
of the Bangladesh.

Did you read about
the army officer's plea for donor's blood?
It was given willingly by boys
who took the needles in their veins,
and from their bodies
every drop of blood was drained.
No time to comprehend, and there was little pain.

And so the story of Bangladesh
is an ancient one again made fresh
by all who carry out commands
which flow out of the laws
upon which nations stand,
which say to sacrifice
a people for a land.

Bangladesh, Bangladesh.
Bangladesh, Bangladesh.
When the sun sinks in the west
die a million people
of the Bangladesh.

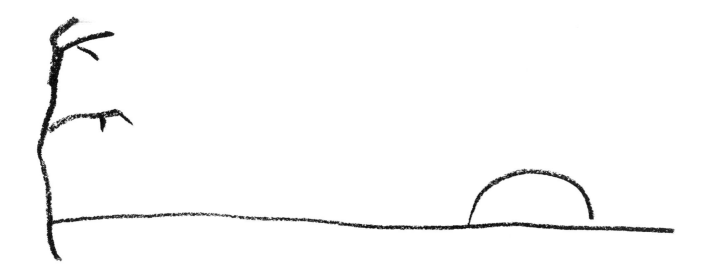

Where Are You Now, My Son?

Words and Music by Joan Baez

It's walking to the battleground
that always makes me cry,
I've met so few folks in my time
who weren't afraid to die.
But dawn bleeds with the people here
and morning skies are red,
as young girls load up bicycles
with flowers for the dead.

An aging woman picks along
the craters and the rubble,
a piece of cloth, a bit of shoe,
a whole lifetime of trouble.
A sobbing chant comes from her throat
and splits the morning air.
The single son she had last night
is buried under her.
  They say that the war is done.
  Where are you now, my son?

An old man with unsteady gait
and beard of ancient white,
bent to the ground
with arms outstretched,
faltering in his plight.
I took his hand to steady him,
he stood and did not turn;
but smiled and wept and bowed
and mumbled softly, "Danke schon."

The children on the roadsides
of the villages and towns
would stand around us laughing,
as we stood like giant clowns.
The mourning bands told whom they'd lost
by last night's phantom messenger.
And they spoke their only words in English,
"Johnson, Nixon, Kissinger."
  Now that the war's being won,
  where are you now, my son?

The siren gives a running break
to those who live in town,
take the children and the blankets
to the concrete underground.
Sometimes we'd sing and joke
and paint bright pictures on the wall,
and wonder if we would die well
and if we'd loved at all.

The helmetless defiant ones
sit on the curb and stare
at tracers flashing through the sky
and planes bursting in air.
But way out in the villages
no warning comes before a blast
that means a sleeping child
will never make it to the door.
  The days of our youth were fun.
  Where are you now, my son?

From the distant cabins in the sky
where no man hears the sound
of death on earth from his own bombs
six pilots were shot down.
Next day six hulking bandaged men
were dazzled by a room of newsmen.
Sally keep the faith.
Let's hope this war ends soon.

In a damaged prison camp
where they no longer had command,
they shook their heads, what irony,
we thought peace was at hand.
The preacher read a Christmas prayer
and the men kneeled on the ground,
then sheepishly asked me to sing
"They Drove Old Dixie Down."
  Yours was the righteous gun.
  Where are you now, my son?

We gathered in the lobby
celebrating Christmas Eve,
the French, the Poles, the Indians,
Cubans and Vietnamese.
The tiny tree our host had fixed
sweetened familiar psalms,
but the most sacred of Christmas prayers
was shattered by the bombs.

So back into the shelter
where two lovely women rose,
and with a brilliance and a fierceness,
and a gentleness which froze
the rest of us to silence
as their voices soared with joy,
outshining every bomb that fell
that night upon Hanoi.
  With bravery we have sung,
  but where are you now, my son?

Oh people of the shelters
what a gift you've given me,
to smile at me and quietly
let me share your agony.
And I can only bow
in utter humbleness and ask
forgiveness and forgiveness
for the things we've brought to pass.

The black pyjama'd culture
that we tried to kill with pellet holes,
and rows of tiny coffins
we've paid for with our souls,
have built a spirit seldom seen
in women and in men,
and the white flower of Bac Mai
will surely blossom once again.
  I've heard that the war is done.
  Then where are you now, my son?

TOMOMFROMGABE

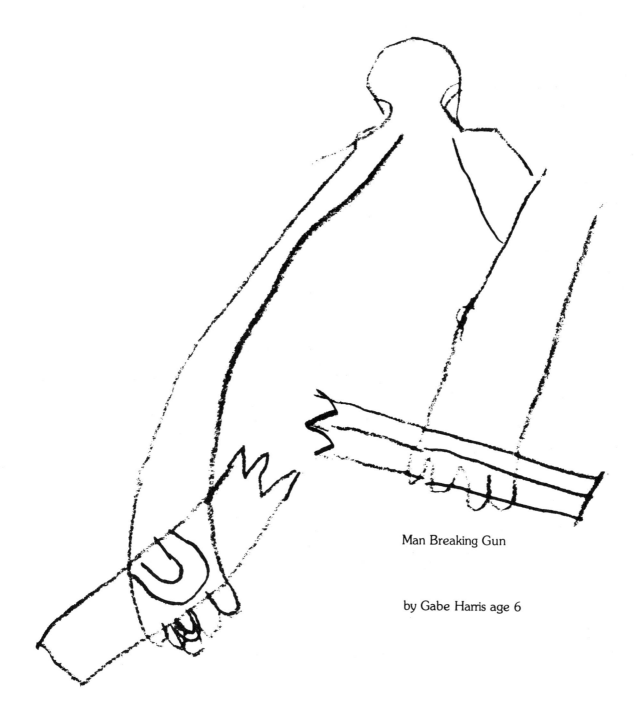

Man Breaking Gun

by Gabe Harris age 6

Only Heaven Knows

Words and Music by Joan Baez

Seems we've been to heaven darling,
ah the sad wind blows.
But I have lost my way my darling,
tell me how it goes.
While the mist is rising darling,
ah the sad wind blows.
Tell me how we met my darling,
tell me all you know.

Well I am somewhat older darling,
ah the sad wind blows.
And you are so much younger darling,
that's the way it goes.
And we looked so good together,
ah the sad wind blows.
Out of all the summer flowers,
I had picked the rose.

Take me in your arms my darling,
while the sad wind blows.
Tell me that this pain will leave me,
tell me how it goes.
Ah if this pain should ever leave me,
only heaven knows.

A Young Gypsy

Words and Music by Joan Baez

A young gypsy fell out in a slumber
heading north with a driver he knew.
Someone he'd lived with and trusted,
a young woman who trusted him too.

That very same day the young gypsy
had come from a farm in the west
where the children had played
through the heat of the day,
affording the gypsy no rest.

And the gypsy's bones were weary
and the front seat looked secure.
And the gypsy slept on
until the sun it was gone,
and the stars pierced the eyes
of the girl at his side.

The next morning's day would be Easter.
He'd dress in his only fine shirt
and shuffle through clusters of strangers
with his gaze and his shoes in the dirt.

And the woman who loved him would watch him,
protect him from curious stares,
for the womenfolk tend to be friendly
and the gypsy's as young as he's fair.

And the evening brought on laughter
and jars of bright red wine.
And the gypsy drank some
and the gypsy had fun,
and his dancing got wild
and the grandmothers smiled.

Sleeping came easily after,
in the arms of the woman that fold
up the secrets and dreams of the gypsy
that will never be sought or be sold.
In fact, they will never be told
for the gypsy is two years old.

Windrose
Instrumental

Rider, Pass By

Words and Music by Joan Baez

Tell me when you see them
gathered at the shore,
dancing on their broken chains.
Ah, the ladies are no more,
in their blue jeans
and their necklaces
against an evening sky.
But some of them are weeping,
crying rider, please pass by.

The ship with all the riders
has drifted out to sea;
compass cracked
and stars unnamed,
it's lost to history.
And the riders in captivity
watch ancient waves roll high,
and hear the distant voices
crying rider, please pass by.

All you men who should have been,
your fathers beat you down.
Your mothers loved you badly,
your teachers stole your crowns.
And the wars you fought
have taken toll,
the price was far too high.
You've buried all the images
of riders passing by.

The horses of the riders
have waited at the tide.
But years have passed,
they know at last,
their heroes will not ride.
So the women oh so gracefully
mount noble horses high,
shattering the timelessness
of rider, please pass by.

But who can dare to judge us,
the women or the men?
If freedom's wings
shall not be clipped,
we all can love again.
So the choice is not of etiquettes,
or finding lonesome ways to die,
but liberty to ships at sea
and riders passing by.
But liberty to ships at sea
and riders passing by.

Dida
Instrumental

Diamonds And Rust

Words and Music by Joan Baez

Well I'll be damned
here comes your ghost again,
but that's not unusual,
it's just that the moon is full
and you happened to call.
And here I sit,
hand on the telephone,
hearing a voice I'd known
a couple of light years ago,
heading straight for a fall.

As I remember your eyes
were bluer than robin's eggs.
My poetry was lousy you said.
Where are you calling from?
A booth in the Midwest.
Ten years ago
I bought you some cuff links.
You brought me something.
We both know what memories can bring,
they bring diamonds and rust.

Well you burst on the scene
already a legend.
The unwashed phenomenon,
the original vagabond,
you strayed into my arms.
And there you stayed
temporarily lost at sea.
The Madonna was yours for free.
Yes, the girl on the half-shell
would keep you unharmed.

Now I see you standing
with brown leaves falling all around
and snow in your hair.
Now you're smiling out the window
of that crummy hotel
over Washington Square.
Our breath comes out white clouds,
mingles, and hangs in the air.
Speaking strictly for me
we both could have died then and there.

Now you're telling me you're not nostalgic.
Then give me another word for it,
you who are so good with words
and at keeping things vague.
Because I need some of that vagueness now,
it's all come back too clearly.
Yes I loved you dearly,
and if you're offering me
diamonds and rust,
I've already paid.

Children And All That Jazz

Words and Music by Joan Baez

Little Annie Fannie
Morgan and Christian
Katy and Nathan
Tommy and Zem Zem
Alex and J.J.
Tai and Ezekiel
Amy and Josie
Matthew and Mosie
Sweet Pearl and Nicholas
come here and tickle us.
I don't like nicknames,
I like to play games.
One of them's Batman,
that's where it's at man.
Look at your T-shirt,
I see you're all wet now.
I'll give you a bath
if you'll go to bed now.
Oh can't you see
I'm tired
I'm tired
I'm tired.

Joey and Janet
Jennifer, Joshua
Justin and Jason
Jacob and Jordan
Heather and Shannon
Marisa and Kirsten
Kimmie and David,
who shall we play with?
Here comes my own son.
Light of my life is
younger than new leaves,
brighter than you please.
Says that he loves me
big as the world,
and Gabriel Harris
you go to bed now,
you go to bed now.
It's quarter to nine
I'm tired
I'm tired
I'm tired.

You heard what I said now,
you go to bed now.
It was a hard day,
never enough play.
Iggy was sick
and couldn't come over.
One of your mice died,
that was when you cried.
Get in the tub
and play with your boats now.
Sit here beside me
I'll tell you a story,
one about snakes
and anything gory.
Ask me no questions,
how far is the sky,
and I'm falling asleep
and you're smarter than I am.
Light of my life
good night
good night
good night.

Winds Of The Old Days

Words and Music by Joan Baez

The lady's adrift
in a foreign land,
singing on issues
both humble and grand.
A decade flew past her
and there on the page
she read that the prince
had returned to the stage.
Hovering near
treacherous waters,
a friend saw her drifting
and caught her.
Unguarded fantasies
flying too far,
memories tumbling
like sweets from a jar.

And take me down
to the harbor now.
Grapes of the summer
are low on the bough.
Ghosts of my history
will follow me there
and the winds of the old days
will blow through my hair.

Breath on an undying ember.
It doesn't take much
to remember
those eloquent songs
from the good old days,
that set us to marching
with banners ablaze.
But reporters
there's no sense in prying,
our blue eyed son's
been denying
the truths that are wrapped
in a mystery.
The sixties are over
so set him free.

And take me down
to the harbor now.
Grapes of the summer
are low on the bough.
Ghosts of my history
will follow me there
and the winds of the old days
will blow through my hair.

Why do I sit
the autumnal judge?
Years of self-righteousness
will not budge.
Singer or savior
it was his to choose,
which of us knows
what was his to lose?
Because idols are best
when they're made of stone,
a savior's a nuisance
to live with at home.
Stars often fall,
heroes go unsung,
and martyrs most certainly
die too young.

So thank you
for writing
the best songs.
Thank you
for righting
a few wrongs.
You're a savage gift
on a wayward bus,
but you stepped down
and you sang to us.

And get you down
to the harbor now.
Most of the sour grapes
are gone from the bough.
Ghosts of Johanna
will visit you there
and the winds of the old days
will blow through your hair.

The Ballad Of Sacco And Vanzetti #1

Lyrics by Joan Baez
Music by Ennio Morricone

"Give to me your tired and your poor,
your huddled masses yearning to breathe free,
the wretched refuse of your teeming shore,
send these, the homeless, tempest-tost to me."

Blessed are the persecuted,
and blessed are the pure in heart.
Blessed are the merciful,
and blessed are the ones who mourn.

The step is hard that tears away the roots
and says goodbye to friends and family.
The fathers and the mothers weep
the children cannot comprehend.
But when there is a promised land
the brave will go and others follow.
The beauty of the human spirit
is the will to try our dreams.
And so the masses teemed across the ocean
to a land of peace and hope,
but no one heard a voice or saw a light
as they were tumbled onto shore,
and none was welcomed by the echo of the phrase,
"I lift my lamp beside the golden door."

Blessed are the persecuted,
and blessed are the pure in heart.
Blessed are the merciful,
and blessed are the ones who mourn.

The Ballad Of Sacco And Vanzetti #2

Lyrics by Joan Baez
Music by Ennio Morricone

Father, yes, I am a prisoner.
Fear not to relay my crime.
The crime is loving the forsaken,
only silence is shame.

And now I'll tell you what's against us:
an art that's lived for centuries.
Go through the years and you will find
what's blackened all of history.
Against us is the law,
with its immensity of strength and power.
Against us is the law!
Police know how to make a man
a guilty or an innocent.
Against us is the power of police!
The shameless lies that men have told
will ever more be paid in gold.
Against us is the power of the gold!
Against us is racial hatred
and the simple fact that we are poor.

My father dear, I am a prisoner.
Don't be ashamed to tell my crime.
The crime of love and brotherhood
and only silence is shame.

With me I have my love, my innocence,
the workers and the poor.
For all of this I'm safe and strong
and hope is mine.
Rebellion, revolution don't need dollars
they need this instead:
Imagination, suffering, light and love,
and care for every human being.
You never steal, you never kill.
You are a part of hope and life.
The revolution goes from man to man
and heart to heart.
And I sense when I look at the stars
that we are children of life.
Death is small.

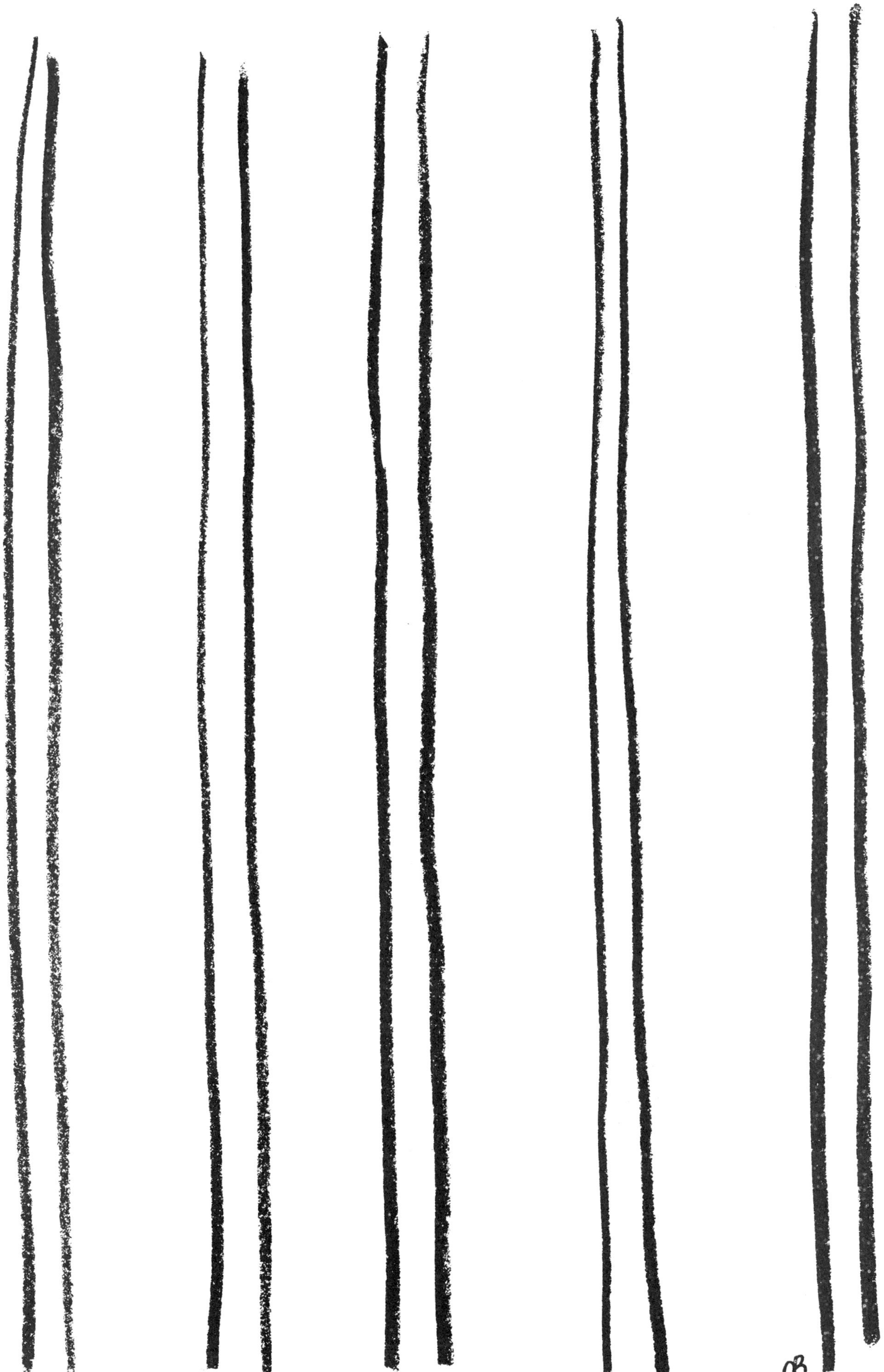

The Ballad Of Sacco And Vanzetti #3

Lyrics by Joan Baez
Music by Ennio Morricone

My son, instead of crying be strong.
Be brave and comfort your mother.
Don't cry for the tears are wasted.
Let not also the years be wasted.

Forgive me son for this unjust death
which takes your father from your side.
Forgive me all who are my friends,
I am with you so do not cry.
If mother wants to be distracted
from the sadness and the soulness,
you take her for a walk
along the quiet country
and rest beneath the shade of trees,
where here and there you gather flowers.
Beside the music and the water
is the peacefulness of nature.
She will enjoy it very much
and surely you'll enjoy it too.
But son you must remember
do not use it all yourself,
but down yourself one little step
to help the weak ones by your side.

Forgive me son for this unjust death
which takes your father from your side.
Forgive me all who are my friends,
I am with you so do not cry.

The weaker ones that cry for help,
the persecuted and the victim,
they are your friends
and comrades in the fight,
and yes they sometimes fall
just like your father.
Yes your father and Bartolo
they have fallen.
And yesterday they fought and fell
but in the quest for joy and freedom.
And in the struggle of this life you'll find
that there is love and sometimes more.
Yes in the struggle you will find
that you can love and be loved also.

Forgive me all who are my friends.
I am with you.
I beg of you, do not cry.

Here's To You

Lyrics by Joan Baez
Music by Ennio Morricone

Here's to you, Nicola and Bart.
Rest forever here in our hearts.
The last and final moment is yours.
That agony is your triumph.

Where's My Apple Pie?

Words and Music by Joan Baez

Been sitting on old park benches,
brother, hasn't it been fun?
But you remember me from the trenches,
I fought in World War One.
Yes, you saw us off at the troop train
smiling a brave goodbye.
But where were you when we came home
to claim our apple pie?

> Oh where's our apple pie
> my friends,
> where's our apple pie?
> We've walked and wheeled
> from the battlefield,
> now where's our apple pie?

World War Two was a favorite,
God was surely on our side.
The teenage kids enlisted with
the blessings of their daddies' pride.
Well the wars may change,
but not so the glaze
in the young boys' eyes
when they cry out for their mamas
in the hours before they die.

> Oh where's our apple pie
> my friends,
> where's our apple pie?
> We've walked and wheeled
> from the battlefield,
> now where's our apple pie?

I volunteered for the last one
and I don't want to moralize,
but somehow I thought
we deserved the best
for the way we threw away our lives.
For we all believed in something,
I know it wasn't very clear.
But I know it wasn't rats
in a hospital room
and a broken-down wheelchair.

> Oh where's our apple pie
> my friends,
> where's our apple pie?
> We've walked and wheeled
> from the battlefield,
> now where's our apple pie?

Yes Johnny finally got his gun
before he got his apple pie.
Now he hasn't got a hand to eat it with
but still he doesn't want to die.
Because he prefers to go on fighting
and let his baby brother know,
when the next time around
the call goes out,
it's "Hell no, we won't go!"

> There'll be no World War Three
> my friends,
> there'll be no World War Three.
> We've walked and wheeled
> from the battlefield,
> there'll be no World War Three.

Sweeter For Me

Words and Music by Joan Baez

Red telephone sitting by my bed
practically bore your name.
Lying alone in the twilight zone
waiting for your call to come in.
Hadn't been for the kid
who was sleeping upstairs
you'd have found me well on my way
on that midnight plane to L.A.

    You suffered sweeter for me
    than anyone I've ever known.

I dared to look into the years
would you still have your wife?
I dared to peer through my tears
could we ever have a life?
Even thought I was pregnant by you
but I didn't care;
I just talked to my son
would he mind another one?

    You suffered sweeter for me
    than anyone I've ever known.

Once more the mist
rolls to the sea
like a hundred
times we've known.
Trees are faded
and the clouds have stopped
where the wind had blown.
How I dread
when the evening comes
and I cannot be
what you want me to be
when you are next to me.

How silent you are
as the veils come down
before my eyes.
Soft and reserved
as you move away
donning your disguise.
While every folk song
that I ever knew
once more comes true
and love grows old
and waxes cold.

    You suffered sweeter for me
    than anyone I've ever known.

Just one favor of you, my love,
if I should die today.
Take me down to where the hills
meet the sea on a stormy day.
Ride a ridge on a snow white horse
and throw my ashes away
to the wind and the sand
where my song began.

    You suffered sweeter for me
    than anyone I've ever known.

Seabirds

Words and Music by Joan Baez

Don't worry about my politics
they are what they are.
I work best when I get some rest.
Right now I'm in a bar
overlooking the whole wide world
(it's over the Pacific).
I've never written
when I was drunk,
this could be terrific!

> And the seabird
> struggles in the wind.
> She topples,
> balances again.

The lady sitting next to me
is gazing in the eyes
of the stranger sitting next to her
who is mouthing truths and lies.
He's actually quite nice I guess
he has an honest look.
He doesn't know I've lost my mind
scribbling in this book.

> And the seabird
> struggles in the wind.
> She topples,
> balances again.

Consumed by the evening's masterpiece,
completely introverted.
From here I could stare down eternity,
leave alone and not feel deserted.
I'm tired of interesting faces
and the dull ones make me weep.
Don't ask me what my sign is,
instant intimacy runs cheap.

The ocean is so bountiful
it spreads from coast to coast.
The winds scale off the whitecaps.
And the things I love the most
come wafting up into my lap
in the colors of the great sunrise:
children holding cupcakes
with paradise in their eyes.

> And the seabird
> struggles in the wind.
> She topples,
> balances again.

Four big pelicans just flew by
the room got very still,
one of them carried the breath of God
tucked way back in his bill.
I know it was the breath of God,
it's the same as the secret of life.
He's carrying it off to the Shah of Iran
to trade it for the end of strife.

> And the seabird
> struggles in the wind.
> She topples,
> balances again.

Caruso

Words and Music by Joan Baez

Infinity gives me chills.
So could the waters of Iceland.
But there's a difference
in finding diamonds in rust
and rhinestones in a dishpan.
Miracles bowl me over
and often will they do so.
Now I think I was asleep till I heard
the voice of the Great Caruso.

Bring infinity home
let me embrace it one more time.
Make it the lilies of the field
or Caruso in his prime.

A friend of mine gave me a tape
she'd copied from a record disc.
It was made at the turn of the century
and found in a jacket labeled "misc."
And midst cellos, harps and flugelhorns
with the precision of a hummingbird's heart
was the lord of the monarch butterflies,
one-time ruler of the world of art.

Bring infinity home
let me embrace it one more time.
Make it the lilies of the field
or Caruso in his prime.

Yes the king of them all was Enrico,
whose singular chest could rival
a hundred fervent Baptists
giving forth in a tent revival.
True he was a vocal miracle,
but that's only secondary.
It's the soul of the monarch butterfly
that I find a little bit scary.

Bring infinity home
let me embrace it one more time.
Make it the lilies of the field
or Caruso in his prime.

Perhaps he's just a vehicle
to bear us to the hills of Truth.
That's Truth spelled with a great big T
and peddled in the mystic's booth.
There are oh so many miracles
that the western sky exposes.
Why go looking for lilacs
when you're lying in a bed of roses?

Bring infinity home
let me embrace it one more time.
Make it the lilies of the field
or Caruso in his prime.

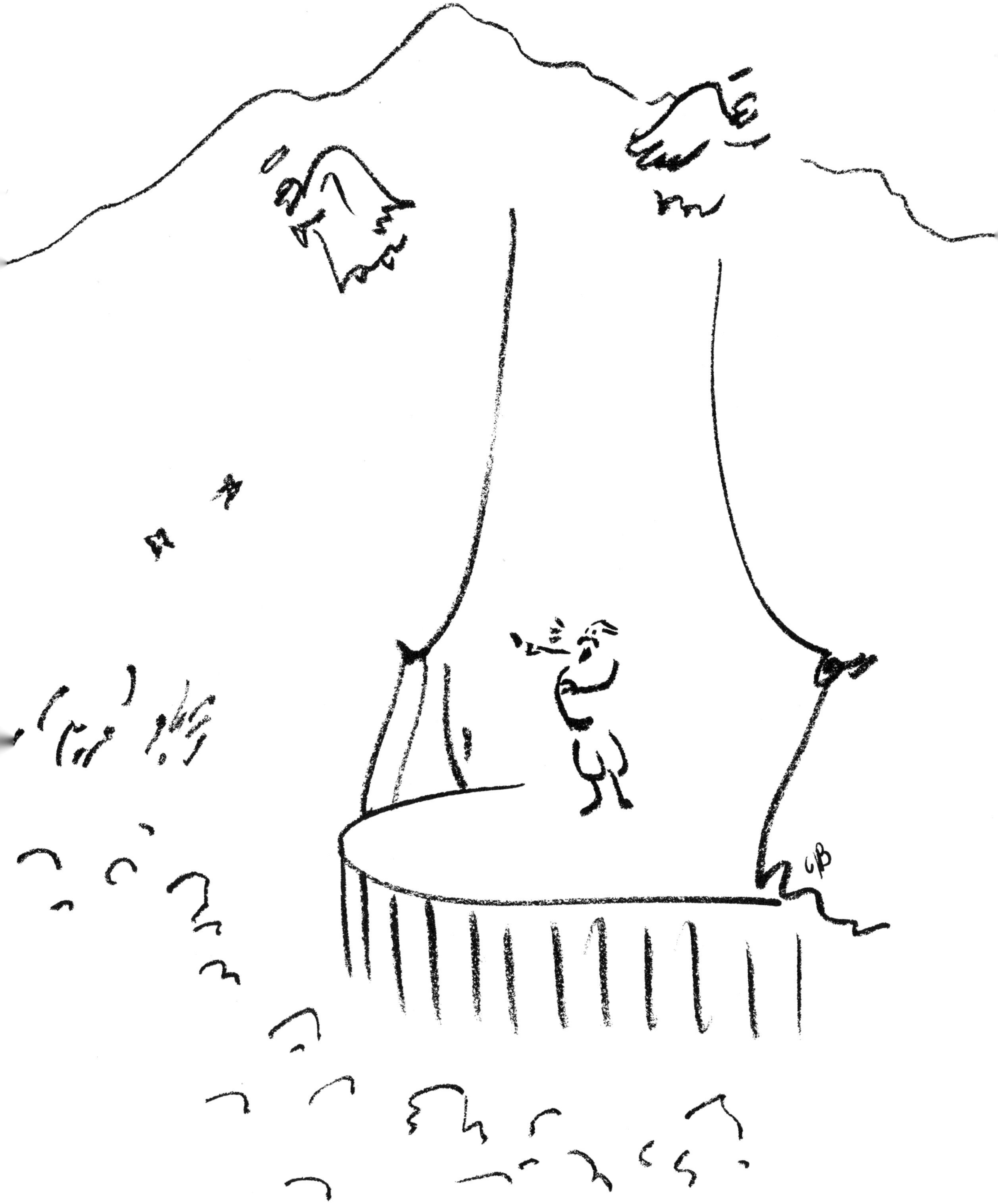

Still Waters At Night

Words and Music by Joan Baez

Still waters at night
in the darkest of dark,
but you rise as white
as the birch tree's bark
or a pale wolf in winter.
You look down and shiver
at still waters at night.

Your eyes are as black
as the blackness you're fearing
and yonder a bridge
and a voice within hearing.
Come walk on me softly
look down and you'll see
still waters at night.

You've reason to fear,
there is no protection
but a garland of emeralds
and a moonlit reflection
of a boat in the distance.
Will the devil take his chance
at still waters at night?

So dance me a small dance
and the night cannot hurt you
nor the waters be silent
nor the emeralds desert you.
For the boat's full of bright scarves
and wild hats among them;
songs of the vagabond
it's to you he has sung them
and shattered the stillness
of still waters at night.

Oh, Brother!

Words and Music by Joan Baez

You've got eyes like Jesus
but you speak with a viper's tongue.
We were just sitting around on earth,
where the hell did you come from?
With your lady dressed in deerskin
and an amazing way about her,
when are you going to realize
that you just can't live without her?

    Take it easy
    take it light
    but take it.

Your lady gets her power
from the goddess and the stars.
You get yours from the trees and the brooks
and a little from life on Mars.
And I've known you for a good long while
and would you kindly tell me, mister,
how in the name of the Father and the Son
did I come to be your sister?

    Take it easy
    take it light
    but take it.

You've done dirt to lifelong friends
with little or no excuses.
Who endowed you with the crown
to hand out these abuses?
Your lady knows about these things
but they don't put her under.
Me, I know about them too,
and I react like thunder.

    Take it easy
    take it light
    but take it.

I know you are surrounded
by parasites and sychophants.
When I come to see you
I dose up on coagulants.
Because when you hurl that Bowie knife
it's going to be when my back is turned
doing some little deed for you,
and, baby, will I get burned.

    Take it easy
    take it light
    but take it.

So little brother when you come
to knock on my door,
I don't want to bring you down
but I just went through the floor.
My love for you extends through life
and I don't want to waste it.
But, honey, what you've been dishing out
you'd never want to taste it.
And if I had the nerve
to either risk it or to break it,
I'd put our friendship on the line
and show you how to take it

    easy
    take it light
    but take it.

Gulf Winds

Words and Music by Joan Baez

It's only when the high winds blow
that I wish my hair was long;
sailing through the autumn leaves
singing an ancient song;
or falling in love in the streets at night
at the edge of a local square.
It's only that I'm here tonight
thinking I was there.

There are high winds on the pier tonight.
My soul departs from me,
striding like Thalia's ghost
south on the murky sea.
And into midnight's tapestry
she fades, ragged and wild,
searching down her ancestry
in the costume of a Persian child.

And gulf winds bring me flying fish
that shine in the crescent moon.
Show me the horizon
where the dawn will break anew.
And cool me here on this lonely pier
where the heron are flying low.
Echo the songs my father knew
in the towns of Mexico.

When I was young my eyes were wise,
my father was good to me.
Instead of having a flock of sons
he had two other girls and me.
And if we had used our Spanish names
here's the way they'd run:
Thalia, Margarita and Juanita.
I'm the middle one.

The screen door kept the demons in
as we moved from town to town.
It's hard to be a princess in the States
when your skin is brown.
And mama smoothed my worried brow
as I leaned on the kitchen door.
Why do you carry the weight, she said,
of the world and maybe more?

And gulf winds bring me flying fish
that shine in the crescent moon.
Show me the horizon
where the dawn will break anew.
And cool me here on this lonely pier
where the heron are flying low.
Echo the songs my father knew
in the towns of Mexico.

My grandfathers were ministers
and it came on down the line.
My father preached in his parents' church
when he was ten years and nine.
And mama dressed in parishoners' clothes
and didn't believe in hell.
Her daddy fought the D.A.R.,
if he'd lived I'd have known him well.

They said go find a Sunday School,
we must have tried them all.
I never stole from the silver plate,
my sisters had more gall.
One preacher said sing out loud and clear,
it's the only life you've got;
and the next one said be good on earth,
you've another life at the feet of God.

And gulf winds bring me flying fish
that shine in the crescent moon.
Show me the horizon
where the dawn will break anew.
And cool me here on this lonely pier
where the heron are flying low.
Echo the songs my father knew
in the towns of Mexico.

My father turned down many a job
just to give us something real.
It's hard to be a scientist in the States
when you've got ideals.
And mama kept the budget book,
she kept the garden too.
Bought fish from the man on Thursday,
fed all of us and strangers too.

But time will pass and so, alas,
will most of what we know.
Though tonight my memory's eye is clear
as the story's being told.
And I'll play ball with the underdog
and sit with the child who's wrong,
be still when the earth is silent
and sing when my strength is gone.

And gulf winds bring me flying
that shine in the crescent moon.
Show me the horizon
where the dawn will break anew
And cool me here on this lonely
where the heron are flying low.
Echo the songs my father knew
in the towns of Mexico.

Now father's going to India
some time in the fall.
They tried to stay together
but you just can't do it all.
I'll think about him if he goes.
There's a little grey in his hair,
though not much because he's Mexic
they don't age they just prepare.

And if he goes to India
I'll miss him most of all.
He'll see me in the mudlark's face,
hear me in the beggar's call.
And mama will stay home I guess
and worry if she did wrong,
and I'll say a prayer for both of them
and sing them both my song.

And gulf winds bring me flying
that shine in the crescent moon.
Show me the horizon
where the dawn will break anew
And cool me here on this lonely
where the heron are flying low.
Echo the songs my father knew
in the towns of Mexico.

Kingdom Of Childhood

Words and Music by Joan Baez

The ship that sails the seven seas
has finally brought me to my knees,
it's not much to my liking.
The people standing on the rock
are innocent and they know not
that the tide comes in,
death rides it like a Viking.

The mountains rise above the mist.
And the golden prince I've never kissed,
he may die tonight.
And why do I want to ride with
the prince whose alleged horse is white?
Because when we ride together
our lives are cloaked forever.

> Happiness is temporary,
> believe me I know.
> It can arrive as a shining crystal
> and leave as the melting snow.
> Come all you lads and lasses.
> The Kingdom of Childhood passes.

Oh but I am hardy in these years,
or I'd have sunk down with my tears
to the earth beneath my feet.
I want to endure the slings and arrows
that Hamlet spoke about but, harrowed,
he was forced to a ragged defeat.

There was a method to his madness
but, overcome by pride and sadness,
he did not endure.
Surely his death was a grave mistake.
How many deaths do we really calculate?
Isn't that true, Lord,
tragedies happen when You're bored?

> Happiness is temporary,
> believe me I know.
> It can arrive as a shining crystal
> or leave as the melting snow.
> Come all you lads and lasses,
> the Kingdom of Childhood passes.

You archangels you have some nerve.
To watch all this you are absurd.
You even have a choice.
Do you know all? I think you may.
And what is there for you to say,
but understand
why God took back your voice.

Silence is golden I believe.
And you are worth your weight
in wreaths of purest gold.
While we are here with debts and bets
and aircraft carriers and jets,
I call out fruitlessly,
give me an archangel for company.

> Happiness is temporary,
> believe me I know.
> It can arrive as a shining crystal
> and leave as the melting snow.
> Come all you lads and lasses,
> the Kingdom of Childhood passes.

Me in the woods at the break of dawn,
the candles of the night still on.
The chimes ring from the hollow.
I too am worth my weight in gold,
but the fishmonger and I are old.
When the mint runs out
our real lives will follow.

If it was misfortune who woke you up
to pour you the dregs from her broken cup,
cast her aside.
The sunrise will appear with the mockingbird
who stays deep in the canyon and is heard
glorious in his song.
He cannot be wrong.

> Happiness is temporary,
> believe me I know.
> It can arrive as a shining crystal
> and leave as the melting snow.
> Come all you lads and lasses,
> the Kingdom of Childhood passes.
> There's another one just beyond,
> act quickly before it's gone.

Time Is Passing Us By

Words and Music by Joan Baez

The moon is low on the southland.
The frogs are asleep on the lake.
Did you know that tears run in rivulets
and hearts can repeatedly break?
And this may well be the last time
if my spirits don't pick up and fly,
for though it is sad
it may well be true,
that our time is passing us by.

Occasionally you have called for me.
I've always tried to be there.
But it seemed whenever my train pulled in
you never did really care.
And the only thing I could decipher
from the corner of your roving eye,
was that you and I
were the first ones to know
that our time was passing us by.

Well it was fun for the first few years
playing Legend In Our Time.
And there were those who discussed the fact
that we drifted apart in our prime.
And we haven't got too much in common
except that we're so much alike.
And I hate it for though
you're a big part of me,
but our time is passing us by.

So I can sit here in my silver chair,
you can stay there on your gold.
You can say you've got commitments,
and I can say I'm growing old.
And I can get up and make comments
on the color of the evening sky,
but our ships have come home
and the night's rolling in
and our time is passing us by.

But cast us adrift
and cross a few stars
and I'm good for one more try.

Stephanie's Room

Words and Music by Joan Baez

"You've loved me exquisitely."
"I tried to."
"Can we be best of friends now?"
"I never lied to you."
"And can I love you forever?"
"Sure," she said, and smiled,
"but will you?"

I wish there was some new way
to sing about a full moon,
poured down on us
like a thousand rivers
in Stephanie's room.
And you said you'd remember always
the shadows on the hills below us.
But will you?

You never once tried
to sell me a bill of goods
that I wouldn't buy.
But I'm seasoned
and I know a pirate
by the devil in his eye.
And the only thing you ever stole from me
was laughter and some love I made,
to fill you.

White snow in the morning
kind of frightened me.
But you'd go sailing anyway,
things are different at sea.
You know I'll never try and change your habit,
as sure as you know if your ship sinks
it'll kill you.

And all the lovely ladies
who came before me
are very much the same
as the others soon to follow
in your merry little game.
I guess I just want to be remembered
especially, and frequently,
like Stephanie.

Five red tail hawks are circling
above us in the sky.
You said they'd bring good luck
and then you said goodbye.
You smiled and said, "I'll see you
sooner than you think,"
but will you?

Luba, The Baroness

Words and Music by Joan Baez

Luba, it was only the finest wine.
Means or no means,
only the finest place to dine.
Paris in the sixties —
you had three sons;
handsome husband by your side,
I flirted with every one.

Your husband, aging but vain,
with the ladies was quite renowned.
Author of books made famous
on his years in the French Underground.
But you, Luba the Baroness,
it was really your blue blood.
No one could touch you with kid gloves
and no one ever should.

    And the hands of little Julian
    will guide you well.
    Et le père du petit Sebastian
    vous attend dans le ceil.*

The youngest son Jerome,
brighter than he could be,
preferred the darkened corners
and was even a little too young for me.
Tall and shy and crafty,
he was oh so scholarly then.
Got married later on,
had a child by the name of Julian.

The eldest Jean François,
what a mixture of sweetness and snobbery,
milkfed by his mother
on Russian aristocracy.
With wits like sabre through silk,
he was the wisest one.
Married and remarried,
had a child by the name of Sebastian.

    And the hands of little Julian
    will guide you well.
    Et le père du petit Sebastian
    vous attend dans le ceil.

Ah my sweet Christophe,
you were only seventeen.
First family dinner with the gypsies,
finger chimes and tambourines.
With candlelit eyes of experience
oh how you laughed at me,
as I became rapidly foolish
under your gaze and on red burgundy.

In sixty nine your father died.
I saw you in the years between.
Handsome, impetuous son of the rich
taking care of your mother, the Queen.
And you are married now as well,
it was inevitable.
Three-day wedding in the south of France,
to an angel named Annabelle.

Recently I was in France,
I called you on the phone.
Caught racing back through memories,
Luba was at home.
Her voice sounded quite the same
as we touched on the amenities.
Suddenly it fell and shattered,
like a thousand broken tiffanies.

In November Jean François died,
we were all there by his side.
Sorry darling that I cried,
it's hard to keep these things inside.
Where are you staying and how is your son?
No we hardly told anyone.
How long are you here, are you with someone?
Hold it, I'll put Christophe on the phone.

Ah my sweet Christophe,
same damn voice.
Hell of a way to become the eldest son,
it's true you had no choice.
And you and Annabelle,
you must take care of her.
Yes I'll be over later on
and I'll bring my guitar.

While going through things afterward,
a letter she wrote and never sent.
A single phrase stood out to you.
These are the words and how it went:

    And the hands of little Julian
    will guide you well.
    Et le père du petit Sebastian
    nous attend dans le ciel.**

*Translation: "And the father of little Sebastian
awaits you in heaven."

**Translation: "and the father of little Sebastian
awaits us in heaven."

Miracles
Words and Music by Joan Baez

Miracles keep happening;
the sun rose in the east today.
I sat up and sighed for the millionth time
as the dawn was phasing a night away.
The blues can last for just so long
and from the depths
there will arise another song.
And I'll sit here in the sea and the sun
waiting for that other song to come.
　　That other song to come.

You don't have to be Black to sing the blues;
from what I gather all you got to be is blue.
Self-indulgence is universal,
adolescence was merely a rehearsal.
Look around you and you will see
everyone has a small franchise on misery.
　　On misery.

　　　And I will sing you a song
　　　just as soon as I get my voice.
　　　When you're up, you're up
　　　and when you're down
　　　you really got no choice.

No rain this winter;
the manzanita reminded me.
We've been living in a drought
and the ocean looks good to me.
Haven't been in love for a year or so,
because I get fussy
and hard to live with as I grow.
Ask the hungry manzanita,
you cannot cross a cypress and a cedar.
　　And a cedar.

My moods are changing, like the sea;
there are a hundred things
that I'd like to be.
Meanwhile I'll sit in the sun,
waiting for that other song to come.
　　That other song to come.

　　　And I will sing it to you
　　　just as soon as I get my voice.
　　　When you're up, you're really up
　　　and when you're down
　　　you really got no choice.

A Heartfelt Line Or Two

Words and Music by Joan Baez

Though the songwriters of the industry
write most of the songs I do,
and it's clear that no one will ever
sing them quite the way I do,
I think tonight I'll sit down and write
a heartfelt line or two,
and if they turn out good enough
I owe every word to you.

To the kid I thought
was a little too young
to know what sadness was,
who took me out when I was down
and set out to find the cause
of why the lady had the blues
and seemed on the verge of tears.
I tell you that kid
must have been around
for a hundred and fifty years.

And to the tough guy blonde
with the front tooth gone
and ships all over his chest,
who approached me out on the promenade
of the beach heading into the west.
His friends lay around
on the muscleman lawn
like a drunken pirate band,
but he turned into a gentleman,
called me a lady
and kissed my hand.

Though the songwriters of the industry
write most of the songs I do,
and it's clear that no one will ever
sing them quite the way I do,
I think tonight I'll sit down and write
a heartfelt line or two,
and if they turn out good enough
I owe every word to you.

To the man and the woman
who threw me a glance
as they picnicked by the sea,
and returned their gaze
to the kid and the food
so as not to bother me.
They got up to leave
and the woman looked on
as the man leaned down to say,
"You've always meant so much to us.
Don't want to bother you
and have a nice day."

And to the band of gypsies
I call friends,
who speak so carefully
to their friend with a life
unlike their own
in its strange complexities.
Who have the patience of the saints
when I've been down for a spell,
I wish it were a whole lot easier
to find the words to wish them well.

Though the songwriters of the industry
write most of the songs I do,
and it's clear that no one will ever
sing them quite the way I do,
I think tonight I'll sit down and write
a heartfelt line or two,
and if they turn out good enough
I owe every word to you.

The Altar Boy And The Thief

Words and Music by Joan Baez

At night in the safety of shadows and numbers,
seeking some turf on which nothing encumbers
the buying and selling of casual looks
stuff that gets printed in X-rated books.
Your mother might have tried to understand
when you were hardly your daddy's little man,
and you gave up saluting the chief
to find yourself some relief.

Finely plucked eyebrows and skin of satin.
Smiling, seductive and endlessly Latin.
Olympic body on dancing feet
perfume thickening the air like heat,
a transient star of gay bar fame
you quit your job and changed your name.
And you're nearly beyond belief
as you hunt down a little relief.

The seven foot Black with the emerald ring
broke up a fight without saying a thing
as the cops cruised by wanting one more chance
to send Jimmy Baldwin back over to France.
And a trucker with kids and a wife
prefers to spend half of his life
in early Bohemian motif,
playing pool and getting relief.

My favorite couple was looking so fine
dancing in rhythm and laughing in rhyme
in the light of the jukebox all yellow and blue
holding each other as young lovers do.
To me they will always remain
unshamed, untamed and unblamed.
The altar boy and the thief,
grabbing themselves some relief.

The altar boy and the thief,
catching a little relief.

Time Rag

Words and Music by Joan Baez

Ripping along
towards middle age
and my music career
kind of missed a page.
Record sales
began to drop
the management all
began to hop.
Not to worry,
they said, you'll see.
What you need is some
fresh publicity.
Just give us a nod
and we'll all leap
towards putting you back
at the top of the heap.
I said, Fine,
I'll give it a whack.
I hung up the phone
and I turned my back.
Began day-dreaming
I was somebody else
when the phone jumped over
from the wall to the shelf.
We just had a break
this is really fine!
We can make the January
issue of Time.
If you'll give us Monday,
a week from today,
from two to four,
now what do you say?

   I said Time,
   Ti:ne mag, mag.
   You got me
   on the rag, rag.
   Take your insults
   about the queen
   and shove them up
   your royal Timese machine.

But I scribbled it down
on the wall calendar
and wondered about
my interviewer.
Maybe he'd be
just a real nice guy
bright and sympathetic
with a roving eye.
We'd forget all about
the assignment due,
formalities, photos,
and the interview.
We'd hop on into
his big rent-a-car;
go for a lovely drive,
not far . . .
maybe France.
As the big day approached
it slipped my mind
till my secretary showed up
at the house to remind me
to switch into gear
for the big coup de gras,
the meeting with the man
from the media.
I swept the driveway
and polished the phone,
put on a Kenzo knit
in two-tone,
fluffed the pillows
in the burgundy chair,
made up my eyes
and brushed my hair . . .
all in that order.
When he called to say
he was three hours late
my cheerful facade
began to disintegrate.
The photographer'd
be even later still:
she was hopelessly lost
in the nearby hills.
He arrived not exactly
the man of my dreams,
not bad for a rep
from the Timese machine.
Asked me a wandering
question or three
and I thought he was
actually listening to me.

   And I said, Time,
   Time mag, mag.
   You got me
   on the rag, rag.
   Take your insults
   about the queen
   and shove them up
   your royal Timese machine.

Curious about his interest
I babbled my way
through the world-wide list:
Ireland, Chile
and the African states,
poetry, politics
and how they relate;
Motherhood, music
and Moog synthesizers,
political prisoners
and Commie sympathizers;
Hetero, homo and bisexuality,
where they all stand
in the nineteen seventies.
Then suddenly it stopped
and he started to lobby,
said, Tell me some inside
stuff about Bobby.
Bobby who? I smiled and said
and the Time man's face
was laced with red.
I know you guys
used to know each other.
I know you refer to him
as being your brother.
And I know that you know
where he's coming from.
I said, You know a lot
for being so Goddamned dumb.

   And I said, Time,
   Time mag, mag.
   You got me
   on the rag, rag.
   Take your insults
   about the queen
   and shove them up
   your royal Timese machine.

Well I never gave him
quite what he came for
the inside story
and it's really a shame
for I never made the
January issue of Time.
And just before I run
out of words that rhyme
I really should tell you
that deep in my heart
I don't give a damn
where I stand on the charts.
Not as long as the sun
sinks into the west
and that's going to be
a pretty serious test
of time.

Juan De La Cruz

Words and Music by Joan Baez

Once again the workers rise with the lark,
there's a Mass going on in the people's park.
Silent and determined they set to embark
on a three day fast and a five mile march,
for a man's been shot on the picket line.
Sixty years of strength was young for dying.
His family is here with eyes of red,
his wife steps down with feet of lead.

    And the sun shines down upon
    the old man whose days are done.
    for a martyr has been taken,
    he is Old Juan de la Cruz.

    And a century of women pray
    at the casket before them laid.
    And the Virgin of Guadalupe
    watches over de la Cruz.

As the heat poured down on the field below,
the lead came a-flying from the vineyard row.
De la Cruz and his wife never ducked or ran,
Union folks since the fight began.
People scattered out laying low to the ground,
and slowly arose as the dust died down.
Birds fluttered soft in his sweet wife's breast
as the bullets sank deep in the old man's chest.

    The tears fell as Cesar read
    the eulogy for the dead.
    And the Bishop broke the people's bread
    over Old Juan de la Cruz.

    In the pitch of night a deal was made,
    the deck's oldest card was played.
    And the devil watched someone get paid
    for the death of de la Cruz.

Thirty years ago in the same damn spot,
the people who ordered the workers shot
fought as the poor for the same damn right
of their children to sleep well fed at night.
Oh Children of the Brotherhood how you've grown,
but the seeds of hate were early sown.
I see that your souls have long since flown
to the river of greed where angels moan.

    Midst flowered veils and weathered graves
    and flags where the great black eagle waves,
    <u>Nosotros Venceremos</u>* plays
    for Old Juan de la Cruz.

    There's work today that must be done.
    Pray for the man who held the gun
    and with sightless eyes shot down the one
    called Old Juan de la Cruz.

The rest of our story now, soft and clear,
how half our daily bread appears.
Picked through the summer by young and old
whose earnings must last through the winter's cold,
by children who have stood with their backs bent down
to scrape the roots from the grower's ground,
and mothers who have wept the night away
for a child born dead on a rainy day.

    Well it's true that blessed are the poor.
    Through an iron mist (I can't be sure)
    it looks like I see heaven's door
    swinging wide for de la Cruz.

    The nuns, the priests and the workers sing,
    through a valley of blood their voices ring.
    Hallelujah, he is risen, and thank you, Lord,
    for Old Juan de la Cruz.

    Hallelujah, he is risen,
    and thank you, Lord,
    for Old Juan de la Cruz.

* Translation: "We Shall Overcome"

Honest Lullaby

Words and Music by Joan Baez

Early early in the game
I taught myself to sing and play
and use a little trickery
on kids who never favored me.
Those were years of crinoline slips
and cotton skirts and swinging hips
and dangerously painted lips
and stars of stage and screen.
Pedal pushers, ankle socks,
padded bras and campus jocks,
who hid their vernal equinox
in pairs of faded jeans.
And slept at home resentfully
coveting their dreams.

    And often have I wondered
    how the years and I survived.
    I had a mother who sang to me
    an honest lullaby.

Yellow, brown and black and white,
Our Father bless us all tonight.
I bowed my head at the football games
and closed the prayer in Jesus' name.
Lusting after football heroes
tough Pachuco little Neroes
forfeiting my A's for zeroes
futures unforseen;
spending all my energy
in keeping my virginity
and living in a fantasy
in love with Jimmy Dean.
If you will be my king, Jimmy Jimmy,
I will be your queen.

    And often have I wondered
    how the years and I survived.
    I had a mother who sang to me
    an honest lullaby.

I travelled all around the world
and knew more than the other girls
of foreign languages and schools,
Paris, Rome and Istanbul.
But those things never worked for me,
the town was much too small you see
and people have a way
of being even smaller yet.
But all the same though life is hard
and no one promised me
a garden of roses, so I did okay.
I took what I could get,
and did the things that I might do
for those less fortunate.

    And often have I wondered
    how the years and I survived.
    I had a mother who sang to me
    an honest lullaby.

Now look at you, you must be growing
a quarter of an inch a day.
You've already lived
near half the years
you'll be when you go away.
With your teddy bears and alligators,
Enterprise communicators,
all the tiny aviators head into the sky.
And while the others play with you,
I hope to find a way with you
and sometimes spend a day with you,
I'll catch you as you fly.
Or if I'm worth a mother's salt,
I'll wave as you go by.

    And if you should ever wonder
    how the years and you'll survive,
    honey, you've got a mother
    who sings to you,
    dances on the strings for you,
    opens her heart and brings to you
    an honest lullaby.

I LOVE
YOU,
GABE.

MOM.

For Sasha
Words and Music by Joan Baez

Here by my window in Germany
a morning bird flies close to me
on his wing I see a yellow star.
The lights are on in the factory
the frost is hung on the Linden tree
and I remember where we are.

And I remember the holocaust.
I remember all we lost.
The families torn and the borders crossed,
and I sing of it now for Sasha.

A young German officer lies in his bed
bandages from toe to head
a prisoner of the camps draws nigh.
If you are Abel and I am Cain
forgive me from my bed of pain,
I know not why we die.
It was I who ordered the building burned,
the job was over and as I turned
a father and his son
caught in the flames high above the ground
from cradled arms the boy looked down
one leap and their lives were done.

And I remember the holocaust.
I remember all we lost.
The children gone and the borders crossed,
and I sing of it now for Sasha.

You in the frozen streets of Heidelberg
your youth unbearded takes form in words
and the ghosts of the past are kind.
For this was your university
the years were long but the spirits free,
and your river runs to the Rhine.
The smoke filled taverns that you once roamed
with the discontented who'd stayed at home
you must have whiskey or you'll die.
The beer garden under the old chateau,
our faces now in the candle glow.
See the memories how they shine.

But you remember the holocaust.
You remember all we lost.
The families torn and the borders crossed,
and we'll sing of it now for Sasha.

Michael

Words and Music by Joan Baez

In the time spent in the foggy dew
with the raven and the dove,
barefoot she walked the winter streets
in search of her own true love.

For she was Mary Hamilton
and lover of John Riley
and the maid of constant sorrow
and the mother of the doomed Geordie.

One day by the banks of the river
midst tears and gossamer,
sweet Michael rowed his boat ashore
and came to rescue her.

> And fill thee up my loving cup
> fast and to the brim.
> How many fair and tender maids
> could love as she could then?

For he was likened to Pretty Boy Floyd
and also John Riley
and a rake and a rambling railroad boy
and the Silkie of the Sule Skerry.

And there in the arms of Michael
in their stolen hour,
loud rang the bells of Rhymney
from the ancient church bell tower.

And there in the night with Michael
while he lay fast asleep,
she put her head to the window pane
and in the fullness of love did weep.

> And fill thee up my loving cup
> fast and to the brim.
> How many fair and tender maids
> will love as she did then?

You've heard of the House of The Rising Sun
and what careless love can do.
You've heard of the wildwood flower
that fades in the morning dew.

And of the ship that circles three times round
and sinks beneath the sea.
You've heard of Barbary Allen,
and now you've heard of me.

> So fill thee up my loving cup
> fast and to the brim.
> How many fair and tender maids
> will ever love again?

Music

For the Guitarist:

The chord progressions indicated above the music are the chords as they sound in the key in which the arrangement is written. Above these are the chord frames and chord names in italics, which are the chords actually played when a capo is used to avoid the more difficult bar chords.

For the guitarist who wishes to play along with the Joan Baez recordings, which are often in different keys than the keys of the piano arrangements, we have supplied a legend above each song, as for example:

Key: E   Capo: 4th   Play: C

This means that Joan Baez sings this song in the key of E; that the capo is to be placed at the 4th fret; that the player is to finger the chords as if they were in C, but that they will actually sound in E.

The legend above the song may also read as follows:

Key: Em   Capo: None   Play: Em

This means that the key of the piano arrangement is the same as the key of Joan Baez's recording. Therefore, the chords may be played with either.

The editors have refrained from suggesting any "picking" styles, preferring to leave that choice up to the guitarist.

See page 4 for Drawings and Poetry

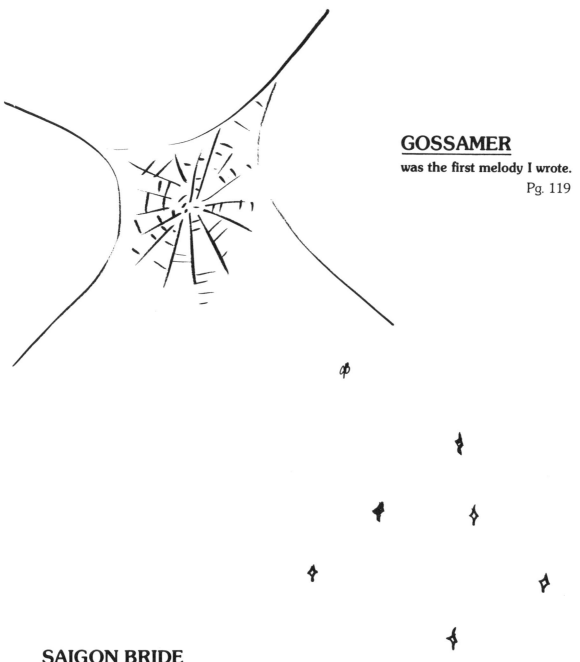

GOSSAMER
was the first melody I wrote.

Pg. 119

SAIGON BRIDE
Like the words to Gossamer, these arrived in the mail from Nina Dusheck, and inspired me to experiment for the second time with picking out a tune on the guitar.

Pg. 123

GOSSAMER

Words by NINA DUSHECK

Music by JOAN BAEZ

KEY: Am   CAPO: NONE   PLAY: Em

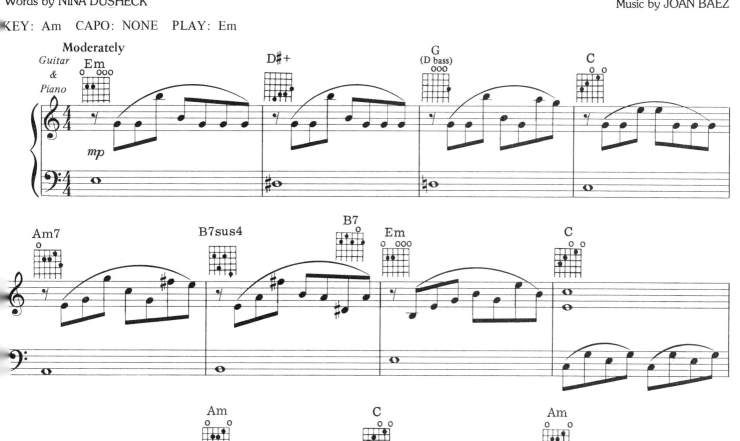

When I was young then all my boughs_____ were thick-ly hung with glit-ter-ing

hopes. But one by one _____ they've blown a - way_____ and on - ly one re - mains to-

til the pat - tern's lost. And one by one_____ hopes blow a -
wa - ter ou - zel's hopes. But one by one_____ they've blown a -
hopes may be re - gained. When I was

way_____ till on - ly one re - mains to - day._____
way_____ and on - ly one re - mains to - day._____

1. I hope the
2. *D. S. al Coda* And when the

Coda young then all my boughs____ were thick - ly

hung with glit - ter - ing hopes. But one by one,_____ they've blown a - way_____ and on - ly

one re-mains to-day. It flut-ters out_____ up-on the

air One hope_ all pinned on Gos-sa-mer._____

SAIGON BRIDE

Words by NINA DUSHECK

Music by JOAN BAEZ

KEY: F CAPO: 3rd PLAY: A

Moderately slow and simply

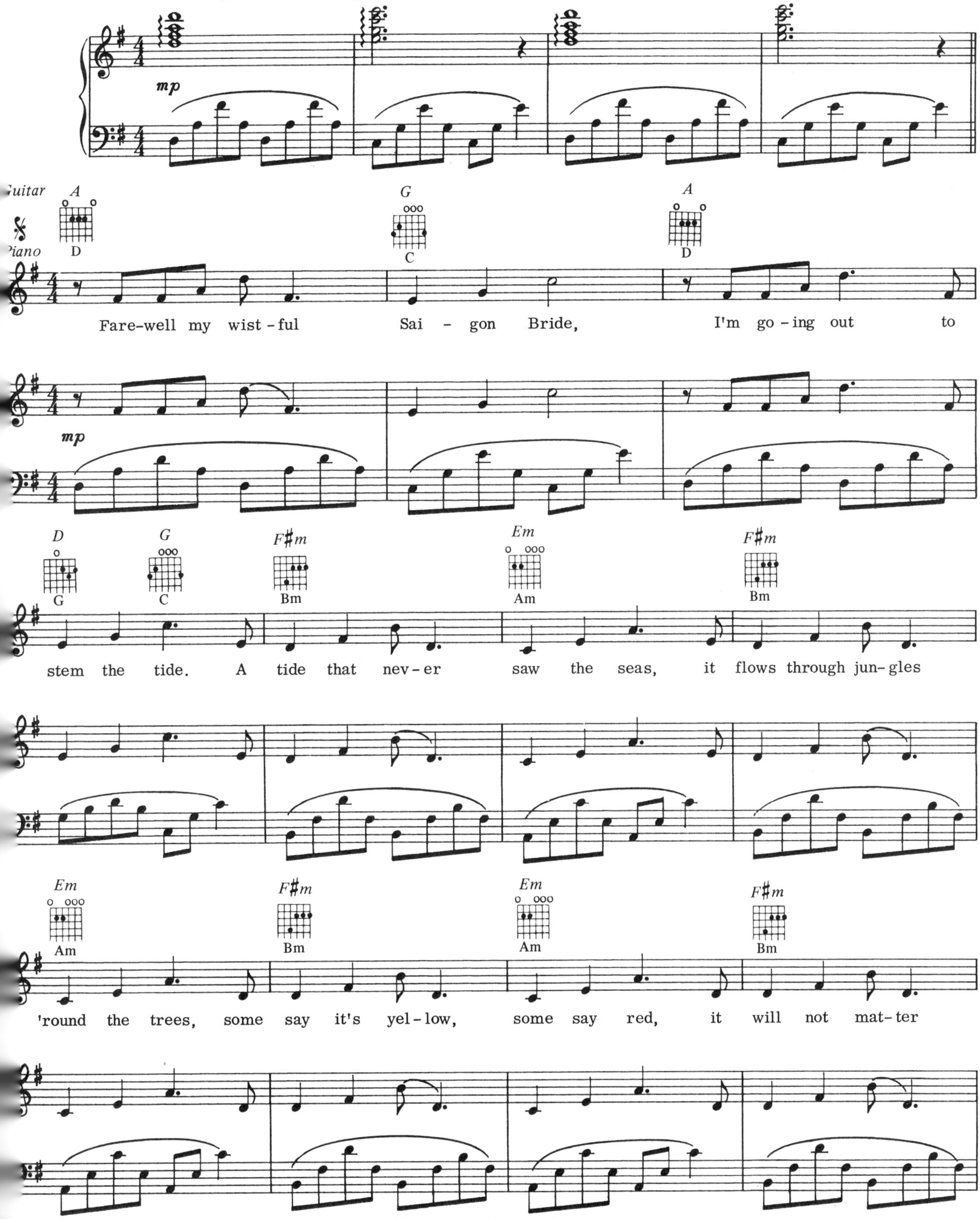
mp
Guitar
Piano
A D
G C
A D
Fare-well my wist-ful Sai - gon Bride, I'm go-ing out to
mp
D G G C
F♯m Bm
Em Am
F♯m Bm
stem the tide. A tide that nev-er saw the seas, it flows through jun-gles
Em Am
F♯m Bm
Em Am
F♯m Bm
'round the trees, some say it's yel-low, some say red, it will not mat-ter

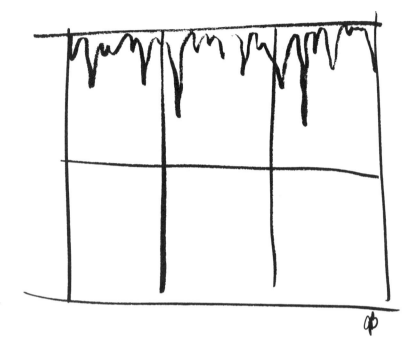

NORTH

The third, and last, song of Nina's I put to music.
Pg. 127

SWEET SIR GALAHAD

took me weeks to write. My first song, really. But it was finished and ready to be sung for my sister Mimi (about whom it was written) at her wedding at the Big Sur Folk Festival, 1968.
Pg. 129

NORTH

Words by NINA DUSHECK

Music by JOAN BAEZ

KEY: Gm CAPO: 3rd PLAY: Em

Moderately slow and tenderly

1. Where i - ci - cles hung
(2.) North
(3.) bird

the blos - soms swing
and the li - lacs bloom
my heart goes forth,

but in my heart
At night they scent
sent by the spring

there my
my
to the

is no spring.
moon - lit room.
shin - ing North.

You were my
You were my
You are my

spring,
spring,
spring,

my sum - mer too,
my sum - mer too,
my sum - mer too,

It's al - ways
I'm go - ing
And I won't

SWEET SIR GALAHAD

Words and Music by JOAN BAEZ

KEY: B CAPO: 4th PLAY: G

130

A SONG FOR DAVID

My way of living out the part of the Vietnam war during which my then-husband was away in prison for draft resistance, and I was pregnant with our son.

Pg. 133

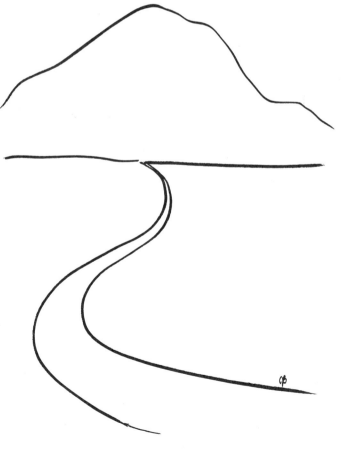

BLESSED ARE...

Thoughts for the parents of young people who have managed to do themselves in on drugs.

Pg. 136

A SONG FOR DAVID

KEY: B   CAPO: 2nd   PLAY: A

Words and Music by JOAN BAEZ

Moderately

1. In my heart _____ I will wait _____ by the ston - y gate, _____
2. (And the) stars _____ in your sky _____ are the stars in mine, _____
3. (And the) hills _____ that you know _____ will re - main for you, _____

_____ And the lit - tle one _____ in my arms _____ will sleep. _____
_____ And both pris - on - ers _____ of this life _____ are we. _____
_____ And the lit - tle _____ wil - low green _____ will stand firm.

_____ Ev - ery ris - ing _____ of the moon _____
_____ Through the same _____ trou - bled wa - ters _____
_____ The flow - ers _____ that we plant - ed _____

2813

BLESSED ARE...

Words and Music by JOAN BAEZ

KEY: C#   CAPO: 1st   PLAY: Dm

2813

138

2813

THREE HORSES

A fantasy song. Your interpretation is probably as valid as mine.

Pg. 141

LAST, LONELY AND WRETCHED

A young soul came to the door. He was terrifying at first; eventually, he drew from me more compassion than fear.

Pg. 145

OUTSIDE THE NASHVILLE CITY LIMITS

Word for word.

Pg. 149

THREE HORSES

KEY: Gm CAPO: 3rd PLAY: Em

Words and Music by JOAN BAEZ

1. In the ear-ly dawn a stal-lion white pranc-es the hills in the morn-ing light,___ His bri-dle is paint-ed with thun-der and gold or-chids and drag-ons pale knights of
2. When the sun is high comes a mare so red Tramp-ling the graves of the liv-ing and dead,___ Her man-tle is heav-y with mir-rors and glass all is re-flect-ed when the red mare does
3. When night does fall comes a stal-lion black So proud and tall he nev-er looks back___ He wears him no em-er-alds sil-ver and gold Not e-ven a cov-er-ing to keep him from

2813

old____ He is the horse____ of the ag - es____ past.____
pass____ She is the horse____ of the here and____ now.____
cold____ He is the horse____ of the years to____ come.____

♪ =126-132

And now the chil-dren run to see the stal - lion on the
And now there is con-fu - sion amongst the chil - dren on the
And I will get me down be - fore this steed up-on my

hill, Bring - ing bags of ap - ples and of clo - ver they have filled,____ And the
hill,____ They cling to one an - oth - er and no long - er can be still,____ While the
knees____ And sing to him the sor - rows of a thou - sand cen - tu - ries.____ And the

white horse____ tells his sto - ries____ of the days now past and gone,____ And the
red mare's____ voice is trem - bling____ with a rare and might - y call,____ The
chil - dren____ now will scat - ter____ as their moth - ers call them home.____ For the

stark____ is the here____ and now.____ known.____ And
I will hang a-bout__ him__ a bell that's nev-er rung____ And thank him for the
man-y words__which from his throat have nev-er sprung And I'll thank God and all the
an - gels__ that the stal - lion of the e-ven-ing,__ the black horse of the
fu - ture_ comes to earth__ but has__ no__ tongue.____

poco rit.

LAST, LONELY AND WRETCHED

KEY: C CAPO: NONE PLAY: A

Moderately in 1

Words and Music by JOAN BAEZ

You're tired _____ and you're poor, _____ you
some - where you were for - sak - en, _____ a -

long to _____ be free, _____ But in this God -
lone, I'll not bear the blame, _____ And some - how _____

for - sa - ken land _____ you find no home, _____ no fam - i -
____ all was tak - en, _____ your mind, your bod - y, your

ly. _____ The man - y roads _____ that you've
name. _____ For - give us _____ our un -

wan - dered _____ since the day _____ of your
kind - ness, _____ our de - ser - tion _____ and our

2813

147

2813

you were well fed.   You laughed and played   till you got

tear - y,   ran to your moth - er   when you were

wea - ry. _____ But

D.S. al Coda

Coda

give us, _____ all the last,   lone - ly and

wretch - ed. _____

OUTSIDE THE NASHVILLE CITY LIMITS

KEY: F CAPO: NONE PLAY: G

Moderately in 2

Words and Music by JOAN BAEZ

1. Out - side the Nash - ville cit - y lim - its, a friend and I did drive. On a day in ear - ly win - ter, I was glad to be a - live. We went to see some friends of his who lived up - on a farm, Strange and gen - tle coun - try folk who'd

2813

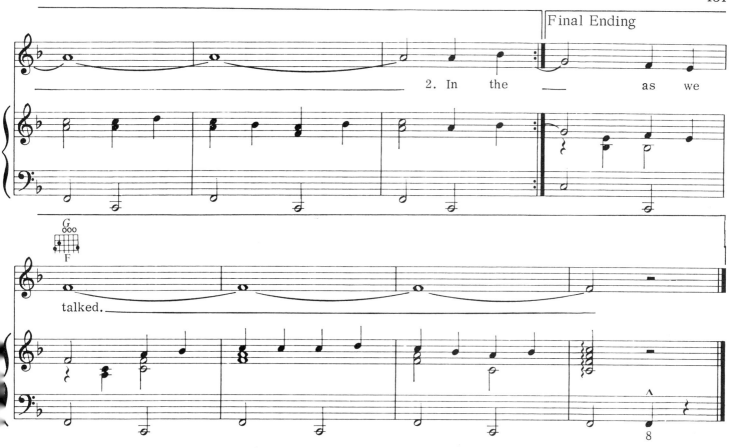

Final Ending

2. In the ___ as we

talked.

2. In the slowest drawl I'd ever heard
   the man said "Come with me
   if y'all wanna see the prettiest place
   in all of Tennessee."
   He poured us each a glass of wine
   and a-walking we did go
   along fallen leaves and crackling ice
   where a tiny brook did flow
   He knew every inch of the land
   and Lord, he loved it so
   But the thing that I remember
   on that cold day in December
   was that my eyes were brimming over
   as we walked.

3. He set me down upon a stone
   beside a running spring
   He talked in a voice so soft and clear,
   like the waters I heard sing.
   He said "We searched quite a time
   for a place to call our own.
   There was just me and Mary John
   And now I guess we're home."
   I looked at the ground and wondered
   how many years they each had roamed
   And Lord I do remember
   on that day in late December
   how my eyes kept brimming over
   as we talked. (As we walked.)

4. And standing there with outstretched arms
   he said to me "You know
   I can't wait till the heavy storms
   cover the ground with snow,
   and there on the pond the watercress
   is all that don't turn white.
   When the sun is high you squint your eyes
   and look at the hills so bright."
   And nodding his head my friend said
   "And it seems like overnight
   that the leaves come out so tender
   at the turning of the winter..."
   I thought the skies they would brim over
   As we talked.

WHEN TIME IS STOLEN
It flies, it flies, it flies. Pg. 153

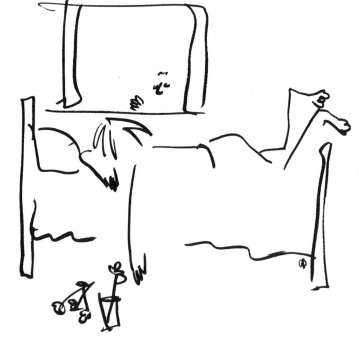

GABRIEL AND ME
Written during early spring dawns when Gabe (my son) was only a few months old.
Pg. 157

MILANESE WALTZ
Movie music with no movie.
Pg. 161

WHEN TIME IS STOLEN

Words and Music by JOAN BAEZ

EY: C   CAPO: NONE   PLAY: C

13

band,　　　　　the　band,　　　the　band.＿＿＿＿＿
track,　　　　　the　track,　　　the　track.＿＿＿＿＿

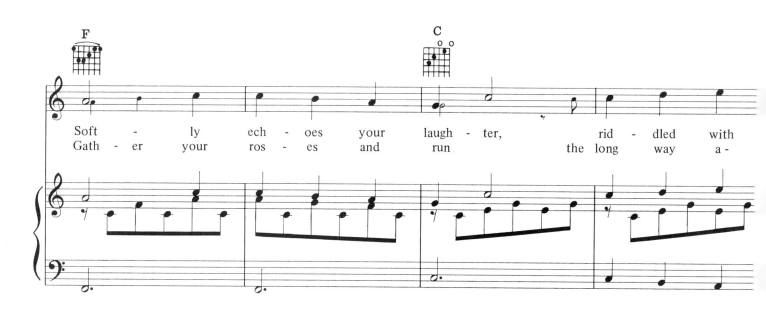

Soft　-　ly　ech　-　oes　your　laugh　-　ter,　　　rid　-　dled　with
Gath　-　er　your　ros　-　es　and　run　the　long　way　a -

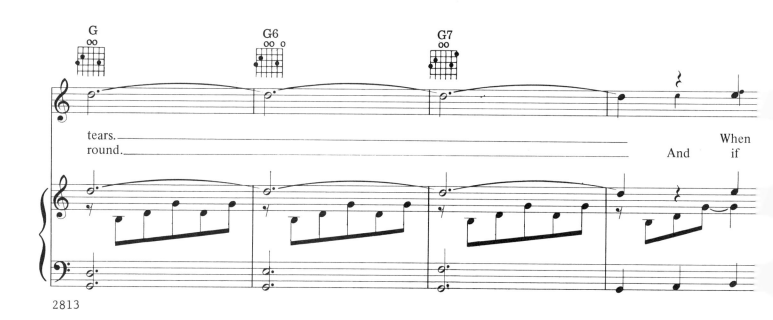

tears.＿＿＿＿＿＿＿＿＿＿＿＿＿＿＿＿＿　　　　　　　When
round.＿＿＿＿＿＿＿＿＿＿＿＿＿＿＿　　And　if

time   is   sto - len   it flies,   it   flies,   it   flies;_____
time   should ev - er be right,   my love,   my   love;_____

_____   Lov - ers   leave in dis - guise,   dis - guise,
I'll   come to   you in the   night,   my   love,

dis - guise,_____   Wea - ri - ness hangs like a   cur - tain,
my   love,_____   But now_____ there's on - ly the   sor - row,

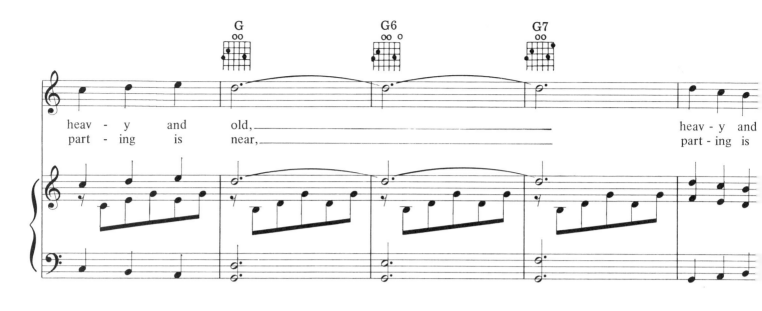

heav - y and old,_____ heav - y and
part - ing is near,_____ part - ing is

cold._____ 2. It's
here,_____

part - ing is here, _____ part - ing is here.

rall.

GABRIEL AND ME

Words and Music by JOAN BAEZ

KEY: C CAPO: NONE PLAY: C

The grey qui - et horse wears the reins of dawn, And His
nose is sil - ver and his mane is white,

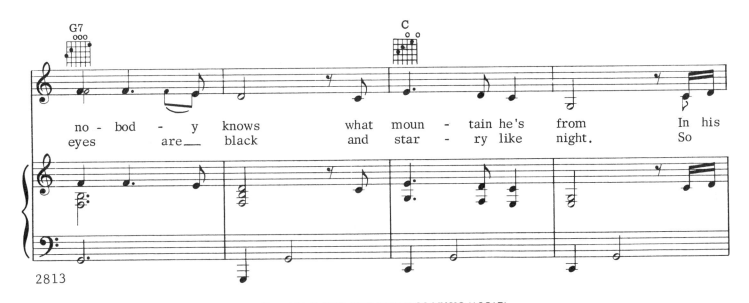

no - bod - y knows what moun - tain he's from In his
eyes are black and star - ry like night. So

2813

mouth he car - ries the gold - en key, And no - bod - y

soft - ly he splash-es his hooves in the sea, That no - bod - y

sees _ him } but Ga - bri - el and me, Ga - bri - el and

hears _ him

me. _____ His _ He _

comes in the morn - ing when the air is still, He rac - es the

back is _ wing - less and there's room for two, We'll mount from a

MILANESE WALTZ

KEY: C CAPO: 3rd PLAY: A

Moderate Waltz Tempo

By JOAN BAEZ

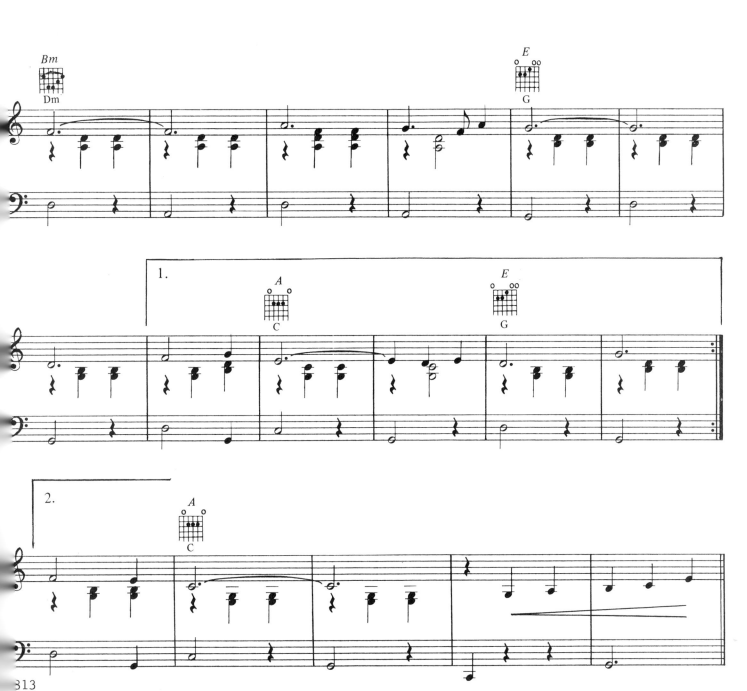

313

162

2813

MARIE FLORE

Yes, Marie is a real person, and she and her family have remained my close friends.

Pg. 165

THE HITCHHIKERS' SONG

Written for my friend Bart, who one day hitchhiked down Highway One in a gold robe to visit me.

Pg. 168

FIFTEEN MONTHS

David had been in jail fifteen of his twenty months.

Pg. 172

MARIE FLORE

Words and Music by JOAN BAEZ

KEY: C CAPO: NONE PLAY: D

Moderately

crowd was the daugh-ter of some-one with flow-ers for me, we were
fit-ted with things from the sev-en-teenth cen-tu-ry and they
shad-ows of a ruin-ed a - re - na her frame in my mind was
flowed with your laugh-ter re - mains to en - light-en the im-age I
there when I'm dream-ing of rain o - ver Par-is, or sun on the

friends at a glance.
suit-ed her well.
nev-er too far.
have of your face.
south end of

In the
For

She spoke no Eng-lish but sat by my side in the car
She would eat noth-ing but sat in her chair like a queen
rush that did fol-low I found she was hold-ing my hand,
I have seen chil-dren with fac-es much wis-er than time,

Point-ing out plac-es en
And laughed at my French but seemed
And ush-er-ing me through an
And you, my Ma - rie, are most

route to the vil-lage of Arles._____ 2. Ma-
al-ways to know what I'd mean._____ 3. Ma-
eve-ning the el-ders had planned._____ 4. Ma-
cer-tain - ly one of this

kind._____ 5. Ma-

France._____

Ma - rie,_____ Ma - rie,_____ Ma-rie

Flore._____

THE HITCHHIKERS' SONG

KEY: A CAPO: 2nd PLAY: G

Words and Music by JOAN BAEZ

FIFTEEN MONTHS

KEY: A CAPO: 2nd PLAY: G

Words and Music by JOAN BAEZ

2813

To Coda ⊕

cold, _____ And the morn - ing's feel - ing
paired _____ And I thank them for
me _____ And I think I'll walk by the

ver - y old. _____
love they've shared. _____
sea a -

Fif - teen months of time _____ my
You see there's real - ly noth - ing wrong, _____ I've just

man's been gone. _____ The sec - ond win - ter
got the blues. _____ Because if _____ you give a

now _____ is com-ing on. _____ And our fates ____ could
damn _____ you're going to pay some dues. _____ But if you see _____ the

all _____ be worse _____ But some-times I
game ____ we're in _____ Like I do, you

still must curse my own. _____
know in time we'll win. _____

And hel - lo _____ I wish you

PRISON TRILOGY
(Billy Rose)

Three true stories David told me during our prison visits. All my prison experiences lead me to believe in the abolition of prisons rather than their reformation.

Pg. 177

LOVE SONG TO A
STRANGER

Life on the road.

Pg. 181

LOVE SONG TO A
STRANGER Part II

More life on the road, from a different perspective.

Pg. 186

PRISON TRILOGY
(Billy Rose)

KEY: A♭ CAPO: 1st PLAY: G

Words and Music by JOAN BAEZ

Moderately, in 2

Bil-ly Rose was a low rid-er Bil-ly Rose was a night fight-er Bil-ly Rose knew trou-ble like the sound of his own name.___ Bust-ed on a drunk-en charge,___ driv-ing some-one else-'s car, the lo-cal mid-night sher-iff's claim to fame.___ In an Ar-i-zo-na jail,___ There are some who tell the tale, how Bil-ly fought the

stuck to the bunk - head, _____ "Don't mess with me, _____ just take me home." _____

_____ Come and lay, _____ help us lay _____ young Bil - ly down. _____

And we'll raze _____ raze the

pri - sons _____ to the ground. _____

But, we're going to raze, ____ raze the pris-ons ____ to the ground. ____

Help us raze, ____ raze the pris-ons ____ to the ground. ____

2. Luna was a Mexican the law called an alien for coming 'cross the border with a baby and a wife
While the clothes upon his back were wet, still he thought that he could get
some money and the things to start a life.
It hadn't been too very long when it seemed like everything went wrong.
Didn't even have the time to find themselves a home
when this foreigner, a brown skinned male thrown inside a Texas jail,
left his wife and baby quite alone.
He eased the pain inside him with a needle in his arm,
but the dope just crucified him and he died to no one's great alarm.
Come and lay, help us lay poor Luna down.
And we'll raze, raze the prisons to the ground.

3. Kilowatt was an aging con of sixty-five who stood a chance to stay alive
and leave the joint and walk the streets again.
As the time he was to leave drew near, he suffered all the joy and fear of leaving thirty-five years
in the pen.
Then on the day of his release, he was approached by the police who took him to the warden
walking slowly by his side,
the warden said you won't remain here but it seems a state retainer claims another
ten years of your life.
He stepped out in the Texas sunlight and the cops all stood around
Old Kilowatt ran fifty yards then threw himself down on the ground.
They might as well just have laid that old man down.
But we're going to raze, raze the prisons to the ground,
Help us raze, raze the prisons to the ground.

LOVE SONG TO A STRANGER

Words and Music by JOAN BAEZ

KEY: C   CAPO: 3rd   PLAY: A

2813

mm.)_____ You stood in the nude_ by the
gone.)_____ Don't tell me of love_ ev-er-

mir-ror and picked out a rose_____ from the bou-quet_____ in our
last-ing and oth-er sad dreams,_____ I don't want_____ to

ho-tel_____ and laid down be-side_ me a-
hear._____ Just tell me of pas-sion-ate

gain, and I watched the rose_____ on the pil-low_____ as
stran-gers who res-cue each oth-er_____ from a life-time_____ of

2813

you gave to me___ oh so man-y things it makes me won-der_____ how

they could_____ be - long to me,_____ and

I gave you on - ly my dark eyes that melt-ed your soul down_____ to the

place where_____ it longs to be._____

LOVE SONG TO A STRANGER Part II

KEY: Am CAPO: NONE PLAY: Am

Words and Music by JOAN BAE

Moderately

2813

2. My thoughts drift in - to the
4. I thought I want - ed to
6. He laughed like I the chimes of a
8. He drank and he cussed and he
10. So here I sit with my

fro - zen night Frank - furt is cov - ered with
mar - ry him His face was sculp - ted by
sil - ver bell His eyes were al - ex - an - drite
wrote his own songs He was ver - y much on the
bas - ket of fruit. And two fin - ger bowls____ of

snow._____ And numb - ly they ride on an
God._____ His words____ were gen - tle an
blue._____ He danced the T'ai Chi with th
go._____ We fol - lowed each oth - er fo
glass._____ I fin - ished my bot - tle o

2813

190

MYTHS
An attempt at a public explanation of the end of a marriage.
Pg. 191

ALL THE WEARY MOTHERS OF THE EARTH
(People's Union #1)
Speaks for itself.   Pg. 195

TO BOBBY
My personal struggle with the apparent fact that Bob Dylan did not share my enthusiasm for street politics.
Pg. 199

MYTHS

KEY: C CAPO: 3rd PLAY: A

Words and Music by JOAN BAEZ

A myth has just been shat-tered,__ up - on the four winds scat-tered,__ back to some sto-ry - book from whence it came.____ Vi- car-i -ous hearts__ may ache,_____ and try to mend the break,_____ and

seek for a right-eous place _____ to put the blame. _____

Nei - ther of us knew _____ what the fu - ture would bring, _____

_____ we on - ly know _____ that now _____ there's some

room to talk and sing. _____ The ba - by laughs _____ a lot _____

194

2813

ALL THE WEARY MOTHERS OF THE EARTH
(People's Union #1)

Words and Music by JOAN BAEZ

KEY: D   CAPO: 2nd   PLAY: C

All the wea-ry moth - ers of the earth will fi - nally rest. We'll— take their ba - bies in our— arms and do our best. When the sun is low up - on the field — to love and mu - sic

2813

they__ will yield,_____ and the wea - ry moth - ers of the earth shall

rest._____ And the

farm - er on__ his trac - tor _____ and be - side his plow, will—
ach - ing work - ers of the world __ a - gain shall sing these—

stand there in con - fu - sion as we wet his brow with the
words in might - y cho - rus - es to all will bring. "We__

TO BOBBY

KEY: C   CAPO: NONE   PLAY: C

Words and Music by JOAN BAEZ

I'll put flow-ers___ at your feet,___ and I will sing___ to you so
say it___ like you said it;___ we'd on-ly try___ and just for-
flow-ers___ at your door,___ and scrib-bled notes___ a-bout the

sweet,___ and hope my words___ will car-ry home___ to your
get it.___ You stood a - lone___ up-on the moun-tain___ till it was
war.___ We're on-ly say - ing___ the time is short___ and there is

heart.___
sink - ing.___
work to do.___

You left us march-ing___ on the
And in a fren-zy___ we tried to
And we're still march-ing___ on the

2813

think _____ your heart was ach - ing,__ or e-ven bro - ken._____ But if

God hears my com - plaint__ He will for - give__ you,_____ and so will I, with all re -

spect,__ I'll just re - live__ you._____ And like - wise you must un-der-stand__

These things we give you:_____ Like these

D.S. al Coda

Coda

dy - ing._____

rit.

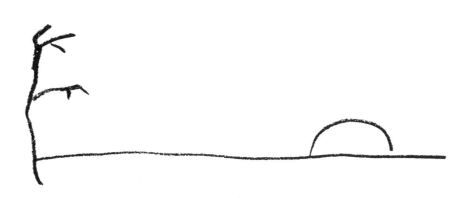

SONG OF BANGLADESH

Again, true stories.

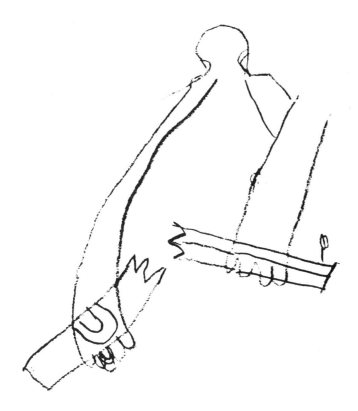

WHERE ARE YOU NOW, MY SON?

If anyone asked me what I thought my "best" work of art was, I would say this documentary of the Christmas bombing in Hanoi was certainly, by its nature, the strongest thing I have ever written.

ONLY HEAVEN KNOWS

Ain't it the truth?

SONG OF BANGLADESH

KEY: Am   CAPO: NONE   PLAY: Am

Words and Music by JOAN BAEZ

Did you read about the army officer's plea
for donor's blood? It was given willingly
by boys who took the needles in their veins,
and from their bodies every drop of blood was drained
No time to comprehend, and there was little pain.

And so the story of Bangladesh
is an ancient one once again made fresh
by all who carry out commands
which flow out of the laws upon which nations stand,
which say to sacrifice a people for a land.

Bangladesh, Bangladesh.
Bangladesh, Bangladesh.
When the sun sinks in the west
die a million people of the Bangladesh.

WHERE ARE YOU NOW, MY SON?

KEY: C CAPO: NONE PLAY: Dm

Words and Music by JOAN BAEZ

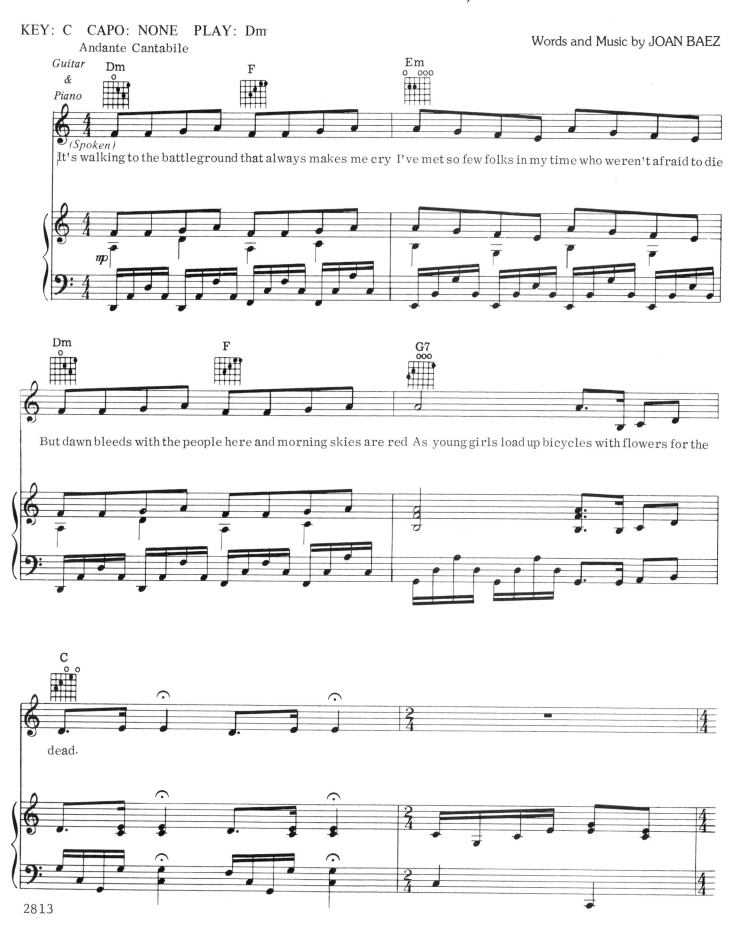

(Spoken)
It's walking to the battleground that always makes me cry I've met so few folks in my time who weren't afraid to die

But dawn bleeds with the people here and morning skies are red As young girls load up bicycles with flowers for the

dead.

2813

An aging woman picks along the craters and the rubble A piece of cloth, a bit of shoe, a whole lifetime of trouble

A sobbing chant comes from her throat and splits the morning air   The single son she had last night is buried under her.

(Sing) They   say____ that the war   is   done

Where____   are you   now,   my   son?_____

1. It's walking to the battleground
that always makes me cry,
I've met so few folks in my time
who weren't afraid to die.
But dawn bleeds with the people here
and morning skies are red,
as young girls load up bicycles
with flowers for the dead.

An aging woman picks along
the craters and the rubble,
a piece of cloth, a bit of shoe,
a whole lifetime of trouble.
A sobbing chant comes from her throat
and splits the morning air.
The single son she had last night
is buried under her.
    They say that the war is done.
    Where are you now, my son?

2. An old man with unsteady gait
and beard of ancient white,
bent to the ground
with arms outstretched,
faltering in his plight.
I took his hand to steady him,
he stood and did not turn;
but smiled and wept and bowed
and mumbled softly, "Danke schon."

The children on the roadsides
of the villages and towns
would stand around us laughing,
as we stood like giant clowns.
The mourning bands told whom they'd lost
by last night's phantom messenger.
And they spoke their only words in English,
"Johnson, Nixon, Kissinger."
    Now that the war's being won,
    where are you now, my son?

3. The siren gives a running break
to those who live in town,
take the children and the blankets
to the concrete underground.
Sometimes we'd sing and joke
and paint bright pictures on the wall,
and wonder if we would die well
and if we'd loved at all.

The helmetless defiant ones
sit on the curb and stare
at tracers flashing through the sky
and planes bursting in air.
But way out in the villages
no warning comes before a blast
that means a sleeping child
will never make it to the door.
    The days of our youth were fun.
    Where are you now, my son?

4. From the distant cabins in the sky
where no man hears the sound
of death on earth from his own bombs
six pilots were shot down.
Next day six hulking bandaged men
were dazzled by a room of newsmen.
Sally keep the faith.
Let's hope this war ends soon.

In a damaged prison camp
where they no longer had command,
they shook their heads, what irony,
we thought peace was at hand.
The preacher read a Christmas prayer
and the men kneeled on the ground,
then sheepishly asked me to sing
"They Drove Old Dixie Down."
    Yours was the righteous gun.
    Where are you now, my son?

5. We gathered in the lobby
celebrating Christmas Eve,
the French, the Poles, the Indians,
Cubans and Vietnamese.
The tiny tree our host had fixed
sweetened familiar psalms,
but the most sacred of Christmas prayers
was shattered by the bombs.

So back into the shelter
where two lovely women rose,
and with a brilliance and a fierceness,
and a gentleness which froze
the rest of us to silence
as their voices soared with joy,
outshining every bomb that fell
that night upon Hanoi.
    With bravery we have sung,
    but where are you now, my son?

6. Oh people of the shelters
what a gift you've given me,
to smile at me and quietly
let me share your agony.
And I can only bow
in utter humbleness and ask
forgiveness and forgiveness
for the things we've brought to pass.

The black pyjama'd culture
that we tried to kill with pellet holes,
and rows of tiny coffins
we've paid for with our souls,
have built a spirit seldom seen
in women and in men,
and the white flower of Bac Mai
will surely blossom once again.
    I've heard that the war is done.
    Then where are you now, my son?

ONLY HEAVEN KNOWS

Words and Music by JOAN BAEZ

KEY: B♭   CAPO: 3rd   PLAY: G

Moderately slow

2813

Tell me how it goes.
That's the way it goes.

While the mist is ris - ing, dar - ling   Ah the sad wind
And we looked so good___ to - geth - er   Ah the sad wind

blows_____
blows_____

Tell me how we met,___ my dar - ling
Out of all the sum - mer flow - ers

Tell me all you know.___
I had picked the rose.___

Well

A YOUNG GYPSY

My sweet gypsy and me on the road down the coast to visit friends.

Pg. 216

WINDROSE

More movie music.

Pg. 221

RIDER, PASS BY

Something to do with giving people permission to fall in love with whomever they please.

Pg. 225

A YOUNG GYPSY

KEY: C   CAPO: NONE   PLAY: C

Words and Music by JOAN BAEZ

A young gyp-sy fell out in a slum-ber_____ Head-ing
next morn-ing's day would be East-er_____ He'd

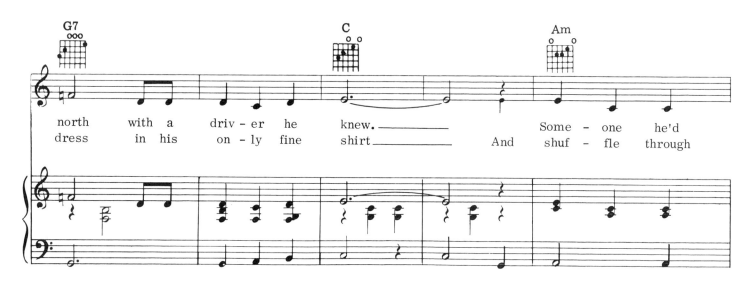

north with a driv-er he knew._____ Some-one he'd
dress in his on-ly fine shirt_____ And shuf-fled through

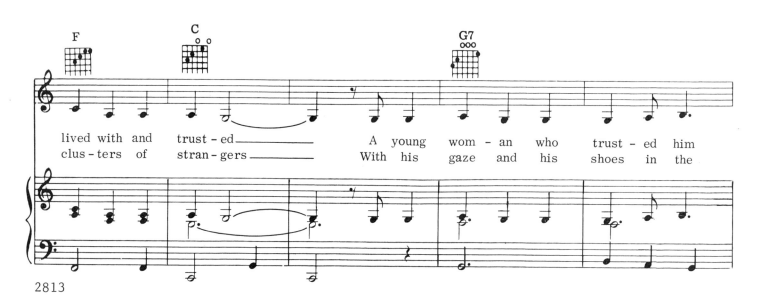

lived with and trust-ed_____ A young wom-an who trust-ed him
clus-ters of stran-gers_____ With his gaze and his shoes in the

too. _____ That___
dirt. _____ And the

ver - y same day the young gyp - sy_____ Had come from a
wom - an who loved him would watch him_____ Pro - tect him from

farm in the west_____ Where the chil - dren had played through the
cu - ri - ous stares_____ For the wom - en folk tend to be

heat of the day, Af - ford - ing the gyp - sy no rest.___
friend - ly And the gyp - sy's as young as he's fair.___

2813

In fact they will nev - er be told _____ For the
gyp - sy _____ is two years old. _____

WINDROSE

KEY: F   CAPO: 3rd   PLAY: D

By JOAN BAEZ

224

2813

RIDER, PASS BY

Words and Music by JOAN BAEZ

KEY: D   CAPO: NONE   PLAY: Bm

Moderately

1. Tell me when you see them gath-ered at the shore danc-ing on their bro-ken chains, Ah, the la-dies are no more In their blue jeans and their

2813

neck-lac-es a-gainst an eve-ning sky_____ But some of them are

weep-ing_____ cry-ing, ri-der, please pass by. by.

Lib-er-ty to ships at sea and ri-ders pass-ing by.

2. The ship with all the riders has drifted out to sea
   Compass cracked and stars unnamed, it's lost to history
   And the riders in captivity watch ancient waves roll high
   And hear the distant voices crying, rider, please pass by.

3. All you men who should have been, your fathers beat you down
   Your mothers loved you badly, your teachers stole your crowns
   And the wars you fought have taken toll, the price was far too high
   You've buried all the images of riders passing by

4. The horses of the riders have waited at the tide
   But years have passed, they know at last, their heroes will not ride
   So the women, oh so gracefully, mount noble horses high
   Shattering the timelessness of rider, please pass by

5. But who can dare to judge us, the women or the men
   If freedom's wings shall not be clipped we all can love again
   So the choice is not of etiquettes, or finding lonesome ways to die
   But liberty to ships at sea and riders passing by,
   Liberty to ships at sea and riders passing by.

DIDA

Instrumental and vocal experimentation.
Pg. 228

DIAMONDS AND RUST

Memories. Pg. 230

DIDA

KEY: D   CAPO: 2nd   PLAY: Cmaj7

Music by JOAN BAEZ

2813

229

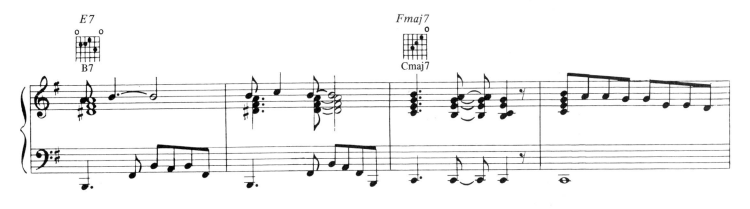

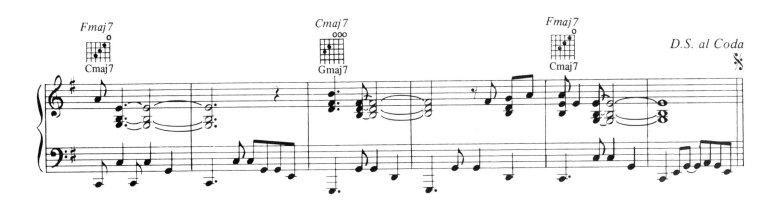

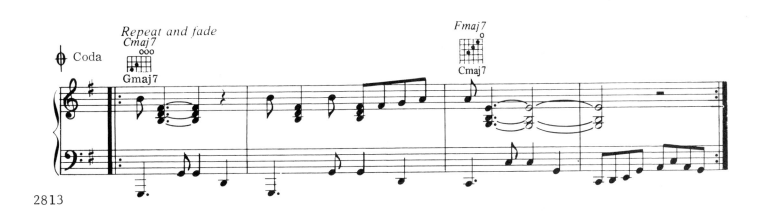

2813

DIAMONDS AND RUST

KEY: Fm   CAPO: 1st   PLAY: Em

Words and Music by JOAN BAEZ

2813

232

2813

Speak-ing strict - ly for me, we both could have died then and there.

D. S. al Coda

Now you're

Coda

Repeat and fade

Repeat and fade

CHILDREN AND ALL THAT JAZZ
A song for mothers.

Pg. 235

WINDS OF THE OLD DAYS
Written for Bob Dylan.

Pg. 240

CHILDREN AND ALL THAT JAZZ

Words and Music by JOAN BAEZ

KEY: D   CAPO: NONE   PLAY: A

Kim-mie and Da - vid _____ Who shall we play _____ with ___

Here comes my own_ son ___ Light of my life _____ is ___

Young-er than new_____ leaves _____ Bright - er than you_____ please _

Says that he loves_ me _____ Big as the world_ and ___

WINDS OF THE OLD DAYS

Words and Music by JOAN BAEZ

KEY: B   CAPO: 4th   PLAY: G

2813

you stepped down_ and you sang to us._____ And get you down to the

har - bor now; most of the sour grapes are gone from the bough. Ghosts of Jo - han - na will

vis - it you there,_ and the winds of the old days will blow___ through your_ hair._____

BALLAD OF SACCO AND VANZETTI #1

Theme song for the Italian film about the Italian immigrants executed for the "crime" of anarchy.

Pg. 252

BALLAD #2

Taken from a letter from Vanzetti.

Pg. 246

BALLAD #3

Taken from Sacco's most famous letter.

Pg. 252

HERE'S TO YOU

This tiny march/hymn has become a peace movement anthem in Europe.

Pg. 253

THE BALLAD OF SACCO AND VANZETTI # 2

Words by JOAN BAEZ

Music by ENNIO MORRICONE

KEY: Am   CAPO: NONE   PLAY: Am

Rather fast in 4

On - ly_____ si - lence is shame._____

And now I'll tell you what's a-
My fa - ther dear, I am a

f passionato

gainst_ us, an art that's lived for cen - tu -
pris - oner. Don't be a - shamed to tell my

13

A - gainst us is the law with its im - men - si - ty of strength and pow - er,_____
With me I have my love, my in - no - cence, the work - ers and the poor,_____

A - gainst us is the law!_____
For all of this, I'm safe and strong and hope is mine.

Po - lice know how to make a man a guil - t - y or an in - no - cent,_____
Re - bel - lion, rev - o - lu - tion don't need dol - lars, they need this in - stead:_____

13

of the gold! _____
man to man _____ and heart to heart.

Dm   E 7   E+   E 7

A-gainst us is the ra-cial ha-tred and the sim-ple fact _____ that we're
And I sense when I look at the stars that we are chil-dren of life.__ Death is

p

Am   1.   2.

poor. _____ My fa - ther
small. _____

2nd time rall. molto

f

13

The Ballad Of Sacco And Vanzetti #1

Lyrics by Joan Baez
Music by Ennio Morricone

''Give to me your tired and your poor,
your huddled masses yearning to breathe free,
the wretched refuse of your teeming shore,
send these, the homeless, tempest-tost to me.''

Blessed are the persecuted,
and blessed are the pure in heart.
Blessed are the merciful,
and blessed are the ones who mourn.

The step is hard that tears away the roots
and says goodbye to friends and family.
The fathers and the mothers weep
the children cannot comprehend.
But when there is a promised land
the brave will go and others follow.
The beauty of the human spirit
is the will to try our dreams.
And so the masses teemed across the ocean
to a land of peace and hope,
but no one heard a voice or saw a light
as they were tumbled onto shore,
and none was welcomed by the echo of the phrase,
''I lift my lamp beside the golden door.''

Blessed are the persecuted,
and blessed are the pure in heart.
Blessed are the merciful,
and blessed are the ones who mourn.

The Ballad Of Sacco And Vanzetti #3

Lyrics by Joan Baez
Music by Ennio Morricone

My son, instead of crying be strong.
Be brave and comfort your mother.
Don't cry for the tears are wasted.
Let not also the years be wasted.

Forgive me son for this unjust death
which takes your father from your side.
Forgive me all who are my friends,
I am with you so do not cry.
If mother wants to be distracted
from the sadness and the soulness,
you take her for a walk
along the quiet country
and rest beneath the shade of trees,
where here and there you gather flowers.
Beside the music and the water
is the peacefulness of nature.
She will enjoy it very much
and surely you'll enjoy it too.
But son you must remember
do not use it all yourself,
but down yourself one little step
to help the weak ones by your side.

Forgive me son for this unjust death
which takes your father from your side.
Forgive me all who are my friends,
I am with you so do not cry.

The weaker ones that cry for help,
the persecuted and the victim,
they are your friends
and comrades in the fight,
and yes they sometimes fall
just like your father.
Yes your father and Bartolo
they have fallen.
And yesterday they fought and fell
but in the quest for joy and freedom.
And in the struggle of this life you'll find
that there is love and sometimes more.
Yes in the struggle you will find
that you can love and be loved also.

Forgive me all who are my friends.
I am with you.
I beg of you, do not cry.

Words by JOAN BAEZ

HERE'S TO YOU

Music by ENNIO MORRICONE

KEY: C CAPO: NONE PLAY: C

Moderately

Guitar Tacet

2813

WHERE'S MY APPLE PIE?

This was written in response to the bitterness and disillusionment of many Vietnam war veterans.

Pg. 256

SWEETER FOR ME

Other memories.

Pg. 259

SEABIRDS

Written while watching a small bird teetering in the wind on the dock below the bar in which I was getting plastered.

Pg. 263

WHERE'S MY APPLE PIE?

KEY: D   CAPO: 2nd   PLAY: C

Words and Music by JOAN BAEZ

1. Been sit - ting on old park ben - ches,
2. World War Two was a fav - orite,
3. I vol-un - teered for the last one
4. Yeah, John - ny fi-nally got his gun_____

Broth - er has - n't it been fun? But you re - mem - ber me from the
God was sure - ly on our side, The teen - age kids were en -
I don't want to mor - al - ize, But some - how I thought we de -
fore he got his ap - ple pie, Now he has - n't got a hand to_____

tren - ches, I fought in World___ War One. Yes,
list - ed With the blessings of their dad - dy's pride. Well, th
served the best For the way we threw a - way our lives. For
eat it with But still he does - n't want to die. Because

you saw us off at the troop train,
wars may change but not so
we all be - lieved in some - thing,

Smil - ing a brave good -
The blaze in the young boys'
I know it was - n't ver - y

bye,
eyes
clear,
know

But where were____ you when we came home To
When they cry____ out for their ma - mas In the
But I know it was - n't rats in a hos - pi - tal room And a
When the next time____ around the call goes out It's

claim our ap - ple pie?____
hours be - fore____ they die.____
bro - ken down____ wheel chair.____
"Hell, no, we____ won't go!"____

1.2.3. Oh,

4. There'll

rall.

D. C. for additional words

SWEETER FOR ME

Words and Music by JOAN BAEZ

KEY: C CAPO: NONE PLAY: C

Slowly

Guitar & Piano Verse — Freely

C   Em

1. Red tel - e - phone sit - ting by my bed_   prac - ti - cally bore_
2. I dared to look_ in - to the years,-   would you still_
* 3. Once more the mist_ rolls to the sea,-   like a hun - dred_
* 4. How silent you are_ as the veils come down_   be - fore_
5. Just one fa - vor of you, my love,_   if I should die_

3rd & 4th verses are sung consecutively.

813

Copyright © 1976, 1977 GABRIEL EARL MUSIC (ASCAP)

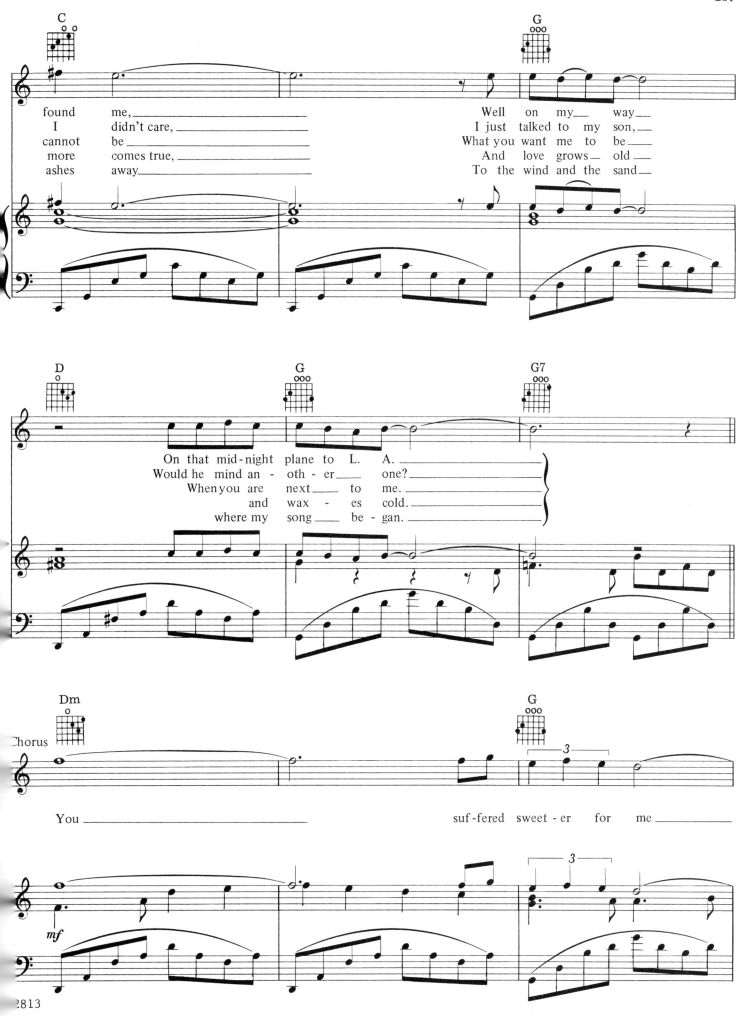

found me,_____
I didn't care,_____
cannot be _____
more comes true,_____
ashes away_____

Well on my___ way___
I just talked to my son,___
What you want me to be___
And love grows___ old___
To the wind and the sand___

On that mid-night plane to L. A._____
Would he mind an - oth - er___ one?_____
When you are next___ to me._____
and wax - es cold._____
where my song___ be - gan._____

Chorus

You _____   suf-fered sweet - er for me_____

SEABIRDS

Words and Music by JOAN BAEZ

KEY: Am   CAPO: NONE   PLAY: Am7

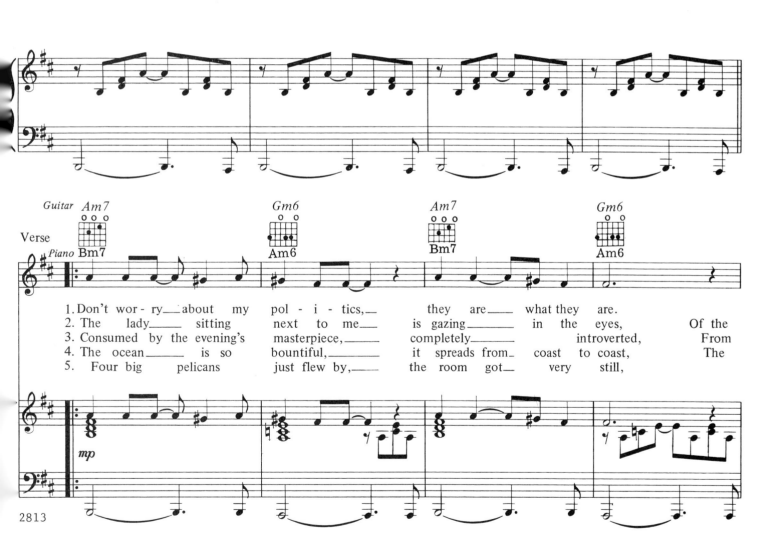

1. Don't wor - ry____ about my pol - i - tics,____ they are____ what they are.
2. The lady____ sitting next to me____ is gazing_____ in the eyes, Of the
3. Consumed by the evening's masterpiece,_____ completely_____ introverted, From
4. The ocean____ is so bountiful,_____ it spreads from____ coast to coast, The
5. Four big pelicans just flew by,____ the room got____ very still,

2813

And the sea - bird ___ strug-gles in the wind, ___ She top - ples, ___
bal - anc - es a - gain. ___

CARUSO

Homage to the great Enrico Caruso, my favorite singer.

STILL WATERS AT NIGHT

For Sara.

OH, BROTHER!

Took forty minutes to complete this angry little ditty. It's wonderful what adrenalin can do.

CARUSO

KEY: F♯ CAPO: 1st PLAY: C7

Words and Music by JOAN BAEZ

1. In - fin - i - ty_____ gives me chills, so could the wa - ters of Ice-
2. A friend of mine_____ gave _____ me a tape she'd copied from a rec - ord disc,_____
3. Yes, the King of them all was Enrico, whose sing - u - lar chest could ri-
4. Per - haps he's just_____ a vehicle to bear us to the hills of_____

land, But there's a dif - ference in find - ing dia - monds in rust_____ and
_____ It was made at the turn of the_____ cen - tu - ry_____ and
val A hun - dred fer - vent_____ Bap - tists giving
_____ truth That's Truth spelled with a_____ great big T, _____ and

2813

rhine - stones___ in a dish - pan.
found in a jack-et labelled "misc."
forth in___ a tent re - vival.
ped - dled___ in the mystic's booth.

Mir - a - cles bowl me o - ver and
And midst cel - los, harps and flugel horns with the
True he was a vo - cal miracle, but
There are oh,___ so man - y mir - a - cles that the

of - ten will they do___ so,
precision of a hum - ming - bird's___ heart,
that's only sec - on - dar - y,
wes - tern sky ex - pos - es,

Now I think___ I was a-
Was the lord of the___ mon-arch___
It's the soul of the___ mon-arch___
Why go look - ing for___

sleep till I heard the voice of the great Ca - ru - so.___
but - ter - flies,___ one time ruler of the world of art.___
but - ter - fly___ that I find a little bit scar - y.___
li - lacs,___ when you're lying in a bed of ro - ses.___

STILL WATERS AT NIGHT

KEY: G CAPO: NONE PLAY: C

Words and Music by JOAN BAEZ

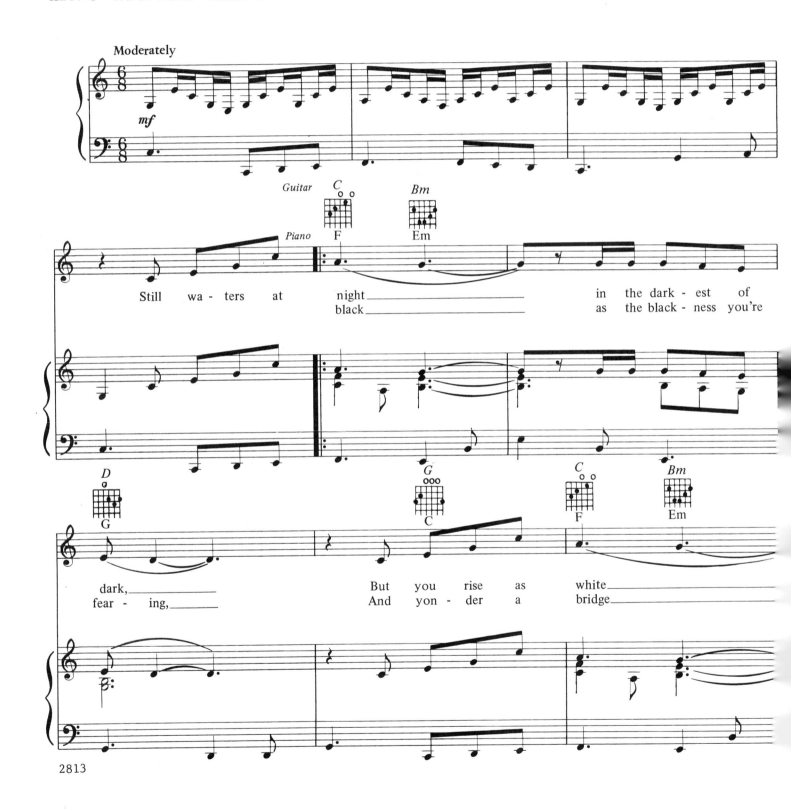

2813

OH, BROTHER!

Words and Music by JOAN BAEZ

KEY: D CAPO: 2nd PLAY: C

2813

honey, what you_ been dish-ing out, you'd nev-er want to taste it. And

if I had the nerve to ei-ther risk it or to break it, I'd

put our friend-ship on the line_ and show you how to take it._____ Take it

GULF WINDS

Written in Corpus Christi perched on a jetty in the Gulf of Mexico. Dedicated to my father.

Pg. 280

KINGDOM OF CHILDHOOD

Fantasies and random thoughts.

Pg. 286

GULF WINDS

KEY: D CAPO: NONE PLAY: D

Words and Music by JOAN BAEZ

1. It's on - ly when the high winds blow that I wish my hair was long,
2. When I was young my eyes were wise, my father was good to me,
3. My grandfathers were ministers and it came on down the line,
4. My father turned down many a job, just to give us something real,
5. Now Father's going to India sometime in the fall,

Sail - ing through the au - tumn leaves, sing - ing an an - cient
Instead of having a flock of sons, he had two other girls and
My father preached in his parents' church, when he was ten years and
It's hard to be a scientist in the States when you've got
They tried to stay together, but you just can't do it

song. Or fall - ing in love in the streets at night at the
me. And if we had used our Spanish names,
nine. And mama dressed in parishioner's clothes and
ideals. And mama kept the budget book, she
all. I'll think about him if he goes, there's

Em   Cmaj7

edge of a lo - cal   square,_____   It's   on - ly   that I'm here to - night__
here's the way they'd run,_____   Thalia,   Margarita   and Juanita.__
didn't believe   in   hell,_____   Her   daddy   fought the D.A.R., if he'd
kept the garden,   too,_____   Bought   fish from the man on Thursday, fed
little grey in his   hair,_____   Though not much, Because he's Mexican, they don't

G   D

think - ing_____   I__ was there.
            I'm the middle one.
lived I'd have known   him well.
all of us   and strangers,   too.
age,   they just   prepare.

There are high__ winds on____   the   pier__   to - night,   my
The   screen_ door kept__ the   demons   in,   as we
They   said,_ go   find_____ a   Sunday   school,   we
But   time_ will pass____ and   so,_   alas,   will
And   if__   he   goes_____ to   India,   I'll

13

Em

fades rag-ged and wild,____
leaned   on the kitchen door,____
only life you've   got,____
sit with the child who's wrong,____
worry if she did   wrong,____

C

Search-ing down her an - ces - try in the
Why do you carry the weight, she said, of the
And the next one said, be good on earth, you've an -
Be still when   the earth is silent   and
And I'll say   a prayer for both of them and

G

cos - tume   of a Per - sian   child.____
world and   maybe   more?____
other life   at the feet of   God.____
sing when   my strength is   gone.____
sing them both   my   song.____

D

Chorus

And

313

KINGDOM OF CHILDHOOD

Words and Music by JOAN BAEZ

KEY: Em   CAPO: NONE   PLAY: C

1. The ship that sails__ the sev-en seas____
2. Oh, but I'm hardy in these____ years, __
3. You archangels, you have some nerve,_____
4. Me in the woods at the break__ of dawn

Has fi-nally brought me to my___ knees;____ it's not much to my lik-
Or I'd have sunk down with my___ tears____ to the earth be-neath my feet.__
To watch all this, you__ are absurd; you even have a choice
The candles of the____ night still on, the chimes ring from the_

The moun-tains   rise___ a - bove the   mist,___
There was a   method   to his   mad - ness,___
Silence is   golden,   I   believe.___
If it was   misfortune   who woke   you   up,

And the Gol - den   Prince I   nev - er___ kissed;___
But   over - come by   pride and___ sadness;___
And   you are   worth your weight in wreaths___
To   pour you the dregs   from her   broken cup___

he   may   die___ to - night.___
he   did   not___ en - dure.___
of   purest   gold.___
cast   her___ aside___

And why
Surely
While
The sunrise

do   I   want   to   ride_____
his   death   was   a   grave mistake,_____
we   are   here with   debts and bets._____
will appear with the   mockingbird_____

With the prince whose al -
How   many
                And
Who   stays   And   deep

leg - ed   horse_   is_   white._____
deaths do   we   really   calculate;_____
aircraft   carriers   and   jets;_____
in the   canyon   and is heard

Because when we ride_ to-
Isn't   that_
I   call out
glorious   in his

geth - er,_____   our lives are cloaked for - ev - er.
true, Lord?_____   Tragedies happen when you're bored.
fruitlessly,   Give me an archangel for   company.
song_____   He cannot   be   wrong.

313

The King-dom Of Child - hood pass - es. There's an -oth- er one

just be - yond,_____ Act quick - ly be - fore it's gone._____

Repeat and fade

TIME IS PASSING US BY

. . .and faster than you think.

STEPHANIE'S ROOM

A love affair in a borrowed room.

LUBA, THE BARONESS

A portrait of a French family.

TIME IS PASSING US BY

KEY: C   CAPO: NONE   PLAY: C

Words and Music by JOAN BAEZ

Moderately

1. The

moon   is low   on the   south - land,_____   the
ca - sion - ally_____   you have   called for   me,_____
it was fun_____   for the   first few   years,_____   play - ing
I   can sit here   in my   sil - ver chair_____

813

STEPHANIE'S ROOM

KEY: Em CAPO: NONE PLAY: Em

Words and Music by JOAN BAEZ

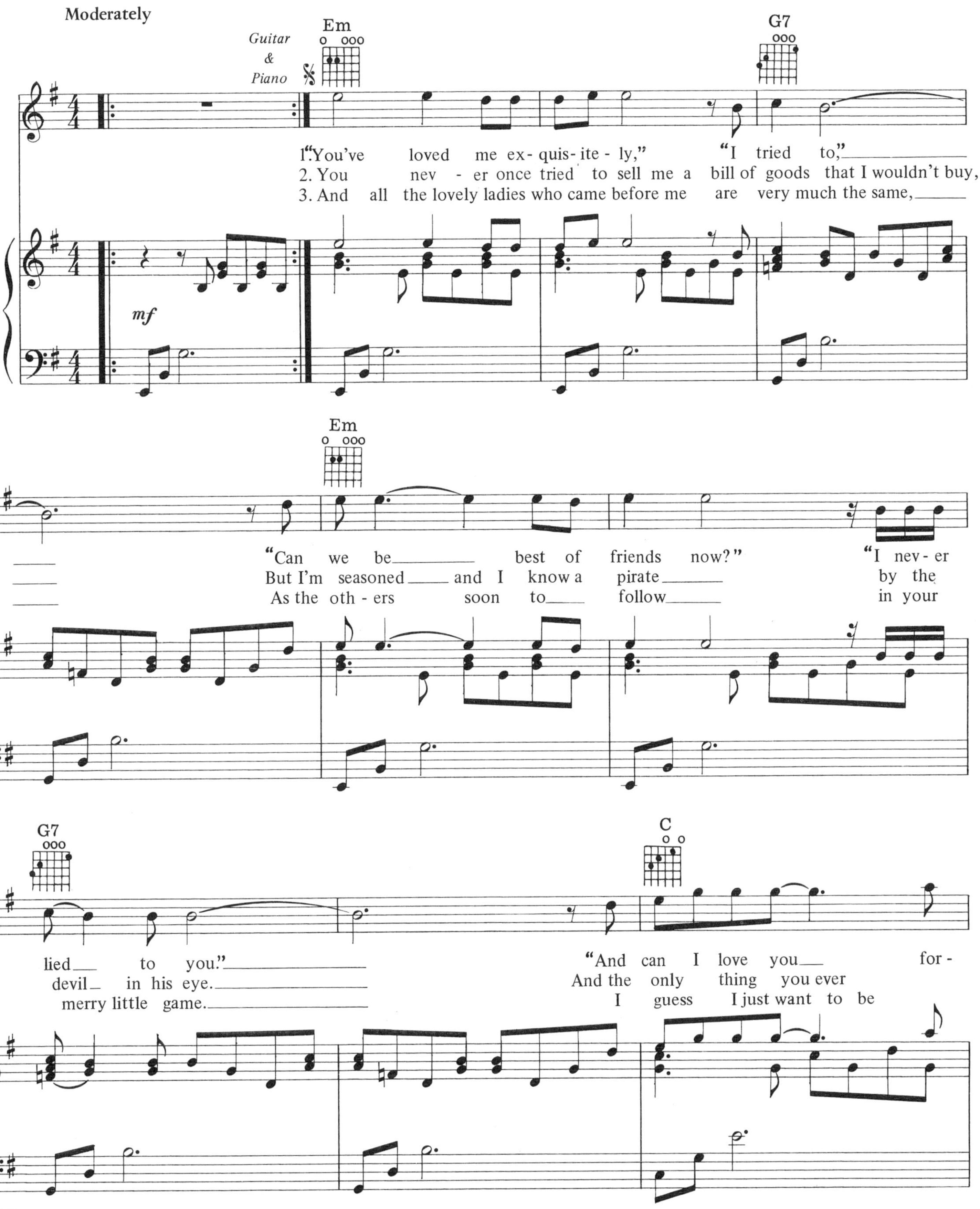
Moderately
Guitar & Piano
Em
G7
C
mf
1."You've loved me ex-quis-ite-ly," "I tried to,"
2. You nev-er once tried to sell me a bill of goods that I wouldn't buy,
3. And all the lovely ladies who came before me are very much the same,
"Can we be best of friends now?" "I nev-er lied to you."
But I'm seasoned and I know a pirate by the devil in his eye.
As the oth-ers soon to follow in your merry little game.
"And can I love you for-
And the only thing you ever
I guess I just want to be

813

But will   you?_____
It'll kill   you._____
But will   you?_____

LUBA, THE BARONESS

Words and Music by JOAN BAEZ

KEY: C# CAPO: 1st PLAY: C

Copyright © 1976, 1978 CHANDOS MUSIC (ASCAP)
Made in U.S.A.

302

place to dine.
young for me.

Pa - ris in the six - ties,
tall and shy and craft - y

you had three sons
he was oh so schol - ar - ly then

Hand-some hus-band by your side,
Got mar-ried lat - er on,

I flirt - ed with ev - ery one.
had a child by the name of Ju - li - an.

2813

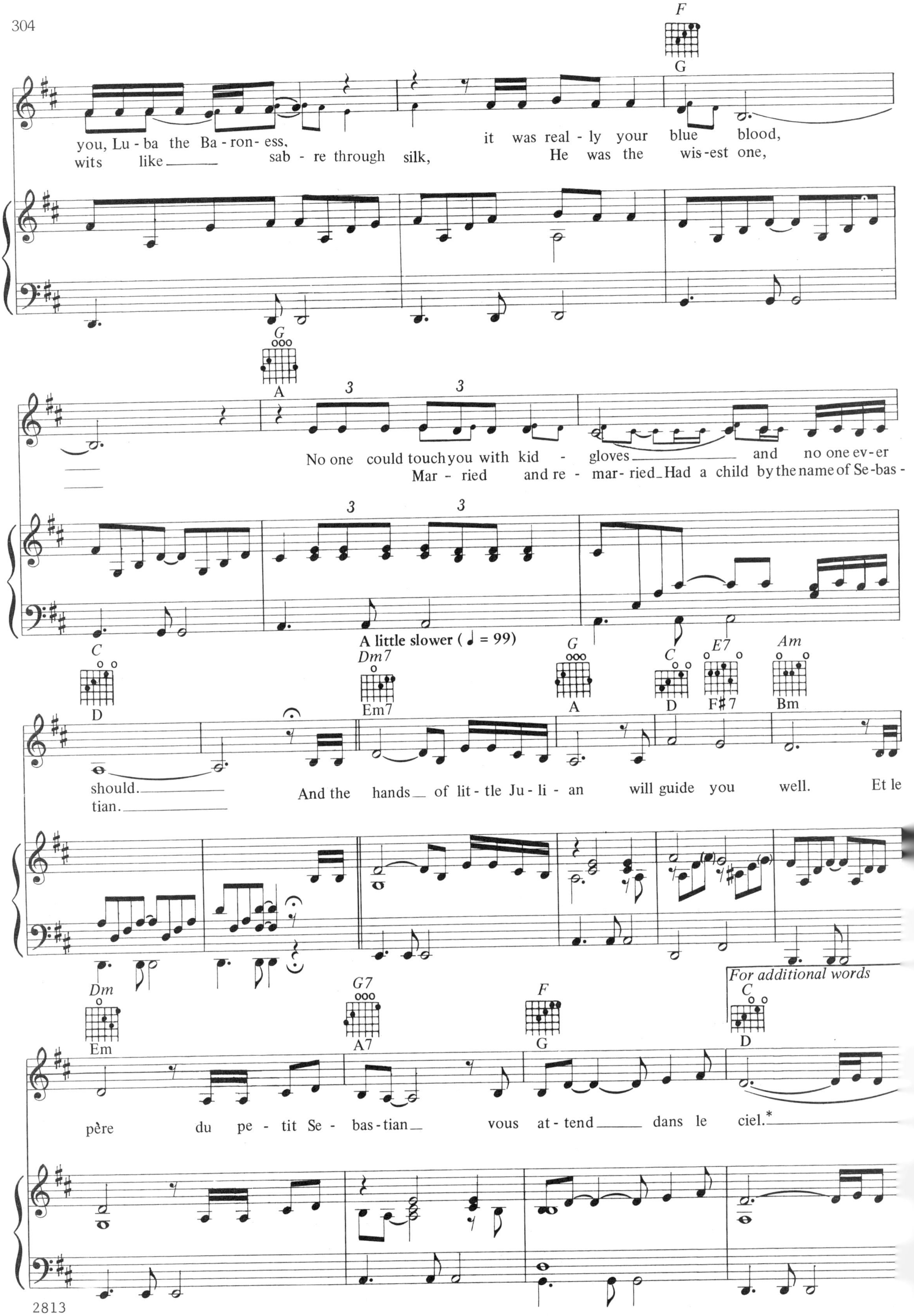
F
G
you, Lu-ba the Ba-ron-ess, it was real-ly your blue blood,
wits like sab-re through silk, He was the wis-est one,
G
A
No one could touch you with kid - gloves and no one ev-er
Mar-ried and re-mar-ried Had a child by the name of Se-bas-
C
D
should.
tian.
A little slower (♩ = 99)
Dm7
Em7
And the hands of lit-tle Ju-li-an will guide you well. Et le
G
A
C
D
E7
F#7
Am
Bm
Dm
Em
père du pe-tit Se-bas-tian vous at-tend dans le ciel.*
G7
A7
F
G
For additional words
C
D

*Translation: "And the father of little Sebastian awaits you in heaven."

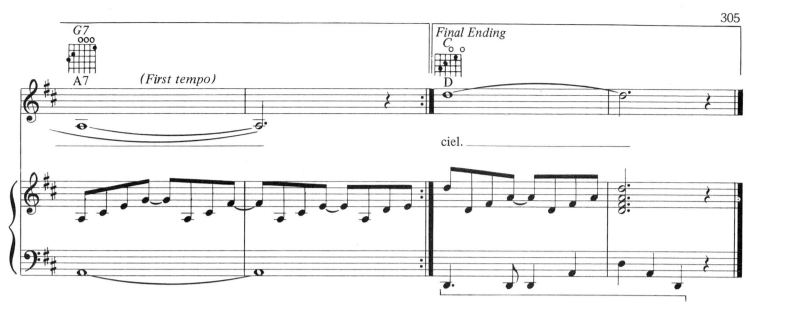

ciel.

Ah, my sweet Christophe, you were only seventeen,
First family dinner with the gypsies, finger chimes and
                              tambourines
With candlelit eyes of experience, oh how you laughed
                              at me,
As I became rapidly foolish under your gaze and on red
                              burgundy.
            In sixty-nine your father died,
            I saw you in the years between,
            Handsome impetuous son of the rich
            Taking care of your mother, the Queen.
And you are married now as well,
            It was inevitable,
Three day wedding in the south of France
            To an angel named Annabelle

Recently I was in France, I called you on the phone,
Caught racing back through memories, Luba was at home.
Her voice sounded quite the same as we touched on the
                              amenities
Suddenly it fell and shattered, like a thousand broken
                              tiffanies
            In November Jean François died
            We were all there by his side,
            Sorry darling that I cried
            Hard to keep these things inside,
            Where are you staying and how's your son
            No we hardly told anyone
            How long are you here, are you with someone,
            Hold it, I'll put Christophe on the phone. . .
Ah my sweet Christophe, same damn voice,
Hell of a way to become the eldest son, it's true you
                              had no choice.
And you and Annabelle, you must take care of her
Yes, I'll be over later on, and I'll bring my guitar.

            While going through things afterward,
            A letter she wrote and never sent,
            A single phrase stood out to you
            These are the words and how it went. . .
It said, the hands of little Julian will guide me well,
Et le père du petit Sebastian nous attend dans le ciel. **

2813

**Translation: "And the father of little Sebastian awaits us in heaven."

MIRACLES
Dedicated to Stevie Wonder.

A HEARTFELT LINE OR TWO
To the people who made me feel good about my songwriting as well as my singing.

MIRACLES

KEY: D CAPO: NONE PLAY: Am9

Words and Music by JOAN BAEZ

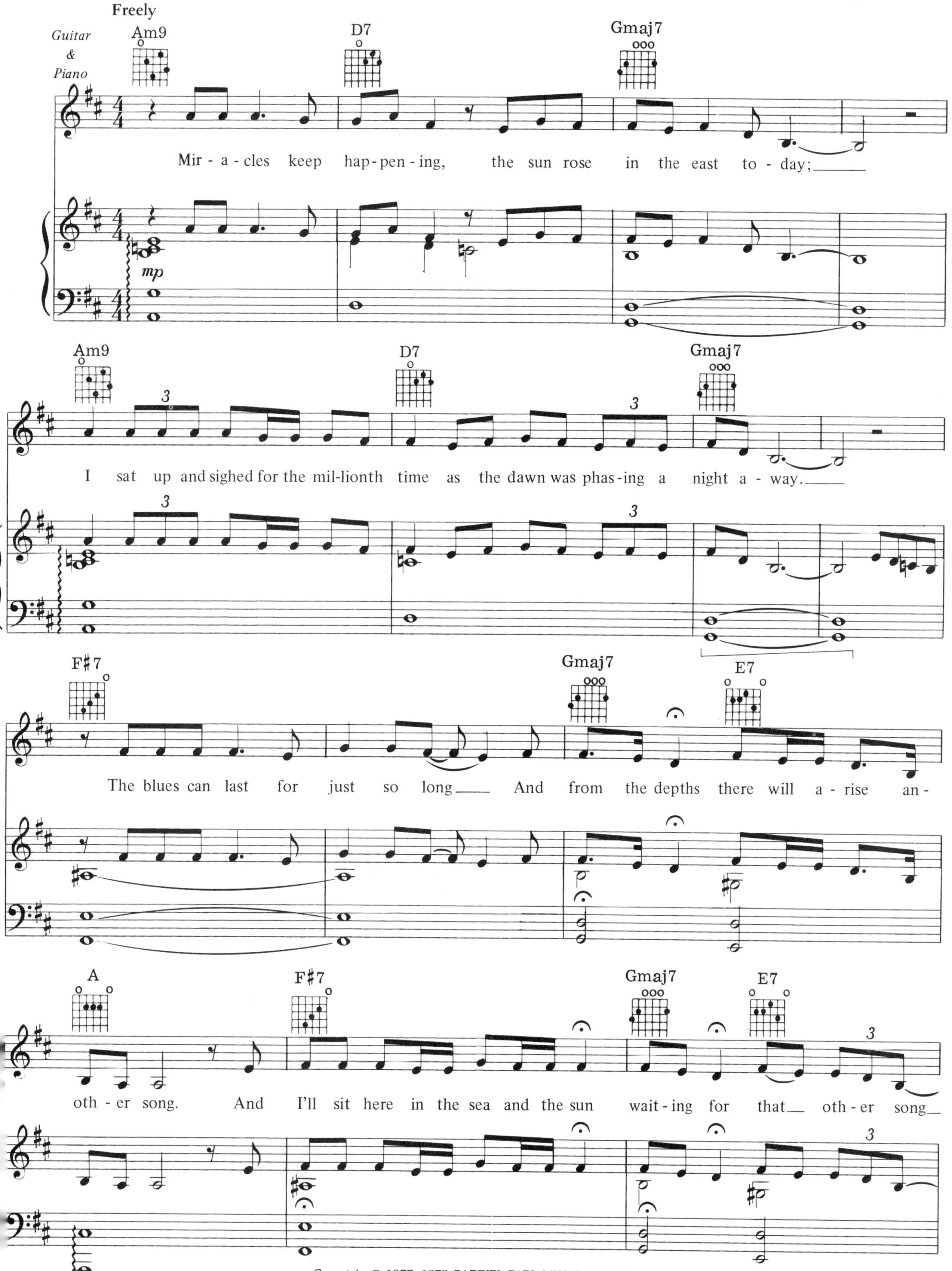
Freely
Guitar & Piano
Am9
D7
Gmaj7
Mir - a - cles keep hap - pen - ing, the sun rose in the east to - day;
mp
Am9
D7
Gmaj7
I sat up and sighed for the mil - lionth time as the dawn was phas - ing a night a - way.
F♯7
Gmaj7
E7
The blues can last for just so long And from the depths there will a - rise an -
A
F♯7
Gmaj7
E7
oth - er song. And I'll sit here in the sea and the sun wait - ing for that oth - er song

In tempo

to come, that oth-er song___ to come.

Moderately

You___ don't have to be Black___ to sing the blues;___
No rain this win-ter the man-zan-i-ta re-mind-ed me;___

From what__ I gath - er all you got to be is blue.___
We've been liv - ing in a drought and the o - cean looks good to me.___

A HEARTFELT LINE OR TWO

KEY: B CAPO: 2nd PLAY: A

Words and Music by JOAN BAEZ

why the la - dy had the blues_ and seemed on the verge of tears_____ I

got up to leave and the woman looked on as the man leaned down to say_____ "You've

tell you that kid must have been a - round for a hun - dred and fif - ty years_____

al - ways meant so___ much to us; don't want to both - er you and have a nice___ day."

___ And to the tough guy blonde with the front tooth gone and ships all o - ver his chest Who ap -

___ And to the band of gyp - sies I call friends who speak so care - ful - ly To their

THE ALTAR BOY AND THE THIEF

A night in a men's gay bar.

Pg. 317

TIME RAG

An attack on the media in general, triggered by an especially distasteful incident with Time Magazine's "Timese Machine," the great editing room which is at the heart of all major popular news media.

Pg. 320

THE ALTAR BOY AND THE THIEF

Words and Music by JOAN BAEZ

KEY: Bb   CAPO: 1st   PLAY: Bm7

Moderately

At night in the safe - ty of shad - ows and num - bers, Seek - ing some turf on which
Fine - ly plucked eye - brows and skin of sat - in, Smil - ing, se - duc - tive and
The sev - en foot Black with the em - er - ald ring___ Broke up a fight with - out
My fav - or - ite cou - ple was look - ing so fine,___ Danc - ing in rhy - thm and

noth - ing en - cum - bers The buy - ing and sell - ing of ca - su - al looks,___
end - less - ly Lat - in, O - lym - pic bod - y on danc - ing feet,___
say - ing a thing___ As the cops cruised by want - ing one more chance_ To
laugh - ing in rhyme_ In the light of the juke box all yel - low and blue,___

2813

319

TIME RAG

KEY: A CAPO: NONE PLAY: A7

Words and Music by JOAN BAEZ

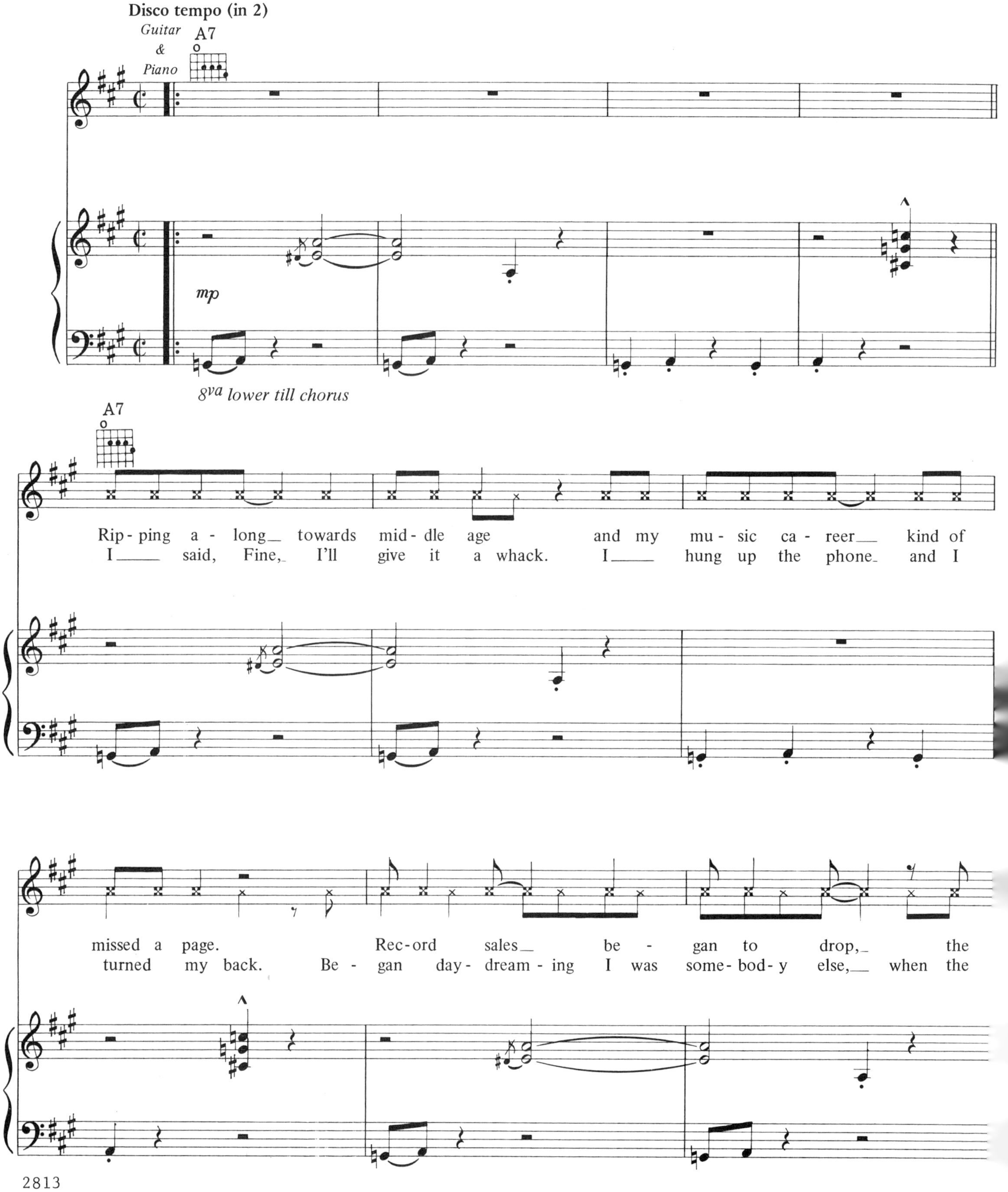
Disco tempo (in 2)
Guitar & Piano
A7
mp
8va lower till chorus
A7
Rip-ping a - long towards mid-dle age and my mu-sic ca-reer kind of
I said, Fine, I'll give it a whack. I hung up the phone and I
missed a page. Rec-ord sales be - gan to drop, the
turned my back. Be - gan day-dream-ing I was some-bod-y else, when the

man - age-ment all___ be - gan___ to hop.___ Not to wor - ry, they said,___
phone___ jumped o - ver from the wall to the shelf.___ We just had a___ break, This is

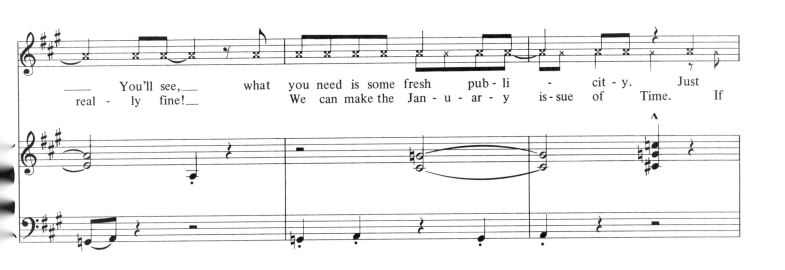

___ You'll see,___ what you need is some fresh pub - li - cit - y. Just
real - ly fine!___ We can make the Jan - u - ar - y is-sue of Time. If

give us a nod___ and we'll___ all leap___ towards put - ting you back___ at the
you'll___ give us Mon - day a week from to - day from two to___ four,___ now

top of the heap.___ I said,
what do you say?___

Chorus

D
Time,_____ Time mag, mag,_____ You

E

D
got me_____ on the rag, rag,_____ Take your

E

D
in - sults _____ a - bout the queen_____ And

C#m

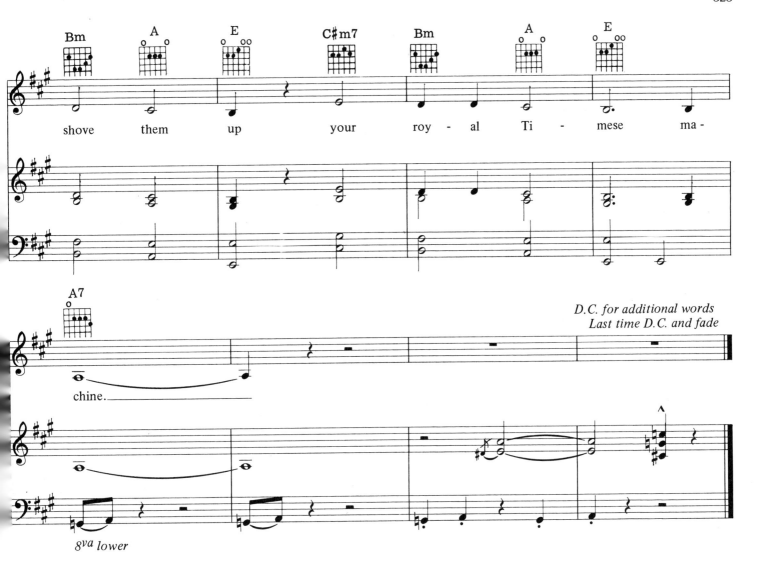

shove them up your roy - al Ti - mese ma- chine.

D.C. for additional words
Last time D.C. and fade

8va lower

But I scribbled it down on the wall calendar
And wondered about my interviewer.
Maybe he'd be just a real nice guy,
Bright and sympathetic with a roving eye,
We'd forget all about the assignment due,
Formalities, photos and the interview,
We'd hop on into his big rent-a-car,
Go for a lovely drive, not far . . . maybe France.

As the big day approached it slipped my mind,
Till my secretary showed up at the house to remind
me to switch into gear for the big *coup de grace*,
The meeting with the man from the media.
I swept the driveway and polished the phone,
Put on a Kenzo knit in two tone,
Fluffed the pillows in the burgundy chair,
Made up my eyes and brushed my hair . . . all in that order.

When he called to say he was three hours late
My cheerful facade began to disintegrate,
The photographer'd be even later still,
She was hopelessly lost in the nearby hills.
He arrived, not exactly the man of my dreams,
Not bad for a rep from the Timese machine.
Asked me a wandering question or three
And I thought he was actually listening to me.
    (Repeat Chorus)

Curious about his interest,
I babbled my way through the world-wide list:
Ireland, Chile and the African states,
Poetry, politics and how they relate.
Mothermood, music and Moog synthesizers,
Political prisoners and Commie sympathizers,
Hetero-, homo-, and bisexuality,
Where they all stand in the 1970's.
Then suddenly it stopped and he started to lobby,
Said, Tell me some inside stuff about Bobby.
Bobby who? I smiled and said,
And the Time man's face was laced with red.
I know you guys used to know each other,
I know you refer to him as being your brother.
And I know that you know where he's coming from. I said,
You know a lot for being so Goddamned dumb.
    (Repeat Chorus)

Well, I never gave him quite what he came for,
The inside story and it's really a shame, for
I never made the January issue of *Time*,
And just before I run out of words that rhyme
I really should tell you that deep in my heart
I don't give a damn where I stand on the charts,
Not as long as the sun sinks into the west,
And that's going to be a pretty serious test
Of time.
    (Repeat Chorus)

JUAN DE LA CRUZ

Juan de la Cruz was a dearly loved member of the United Farm Workers of America. He was killed by Teamster bullets in the summer of 1973, in the struggle for the rights of migrant farm workers.

HONEST LULLABY

Nostalgic song written in the 70's about the 50's and the 80's.

I LOVE YOU, GABE.

MOM.

JUAN DE LA CRUZ

Words and Music by JOAN BAEZ

KEY: Am/A CAPO: NONE: PLAY: Am

Moderately and very steady

Once a - gain the work - ers rise with the lark There's a mass_ go - ing on_ in the

peo - ple's park._ Si - lent and de - ter - mined they set to em - bark On a

three day fast and a five mile march._ For a

Verse 2) As the heat poured down on the field below
The lead came a-flying from the vineyard row
De la Cruz and his wife never ducked or ran
Union folks since the fight began

People scattered out laying low to the ground
And slowly arose as the dust died down,
Birds fluttered soft in his wife's sweet breast
As the bullet sank deep in the old man's chest.

The tears fell as Cesar read
The eulogy for the dead
And the Bishop broke the people's bread
Over Old Juan de la Cruz.

In the pitch of night a deal was made
The deck's oldest card was played,
And the devil watched someone get paid
For the death of de la Cruz.

Verse 3) Thirty years ago in the same damn spot
The people who ordered the workers shot
Fought as the poor for the same damn right
Of their children to sleep well fed at night.

Oh Children of the Brotherhood, how you've grown
But the seeds of hate were early sown
I see that your souls have long since flown
To the river of greed where angels moan

Midst flowered veils and weathered graves
And flags where the great black eagle waves
Nosotros Venceremos plays
For Old Juan de la Cruz.

There's work today that must be done
Pray for the man who held the gun,
And with sightless eyes shot down the one
Called Old Juan de la Cruz.

Verse 4) The rest of our story now soft and clear
How half our daily bread appears,
Picked through the summer by young and old
Whose earnings must last through the winter's cold,

By children who have stood with their backs bent down
To scrape the roots from the growers' ground,
And mothers who have wept the night away
For a child born dead on a rainy day.

Well it's true that blessed are the poor.
Through an iron mist (I can't be sure)
But it looks like I see heaven's door
Swinging wide for de la Cruz.

The nuns, the priests and the workers sing
Through a valley of blood their voices ring,
Hallelujah, he is risen and thank You, Lord,
For Old Juan de la Cruz.

(After last chorus)

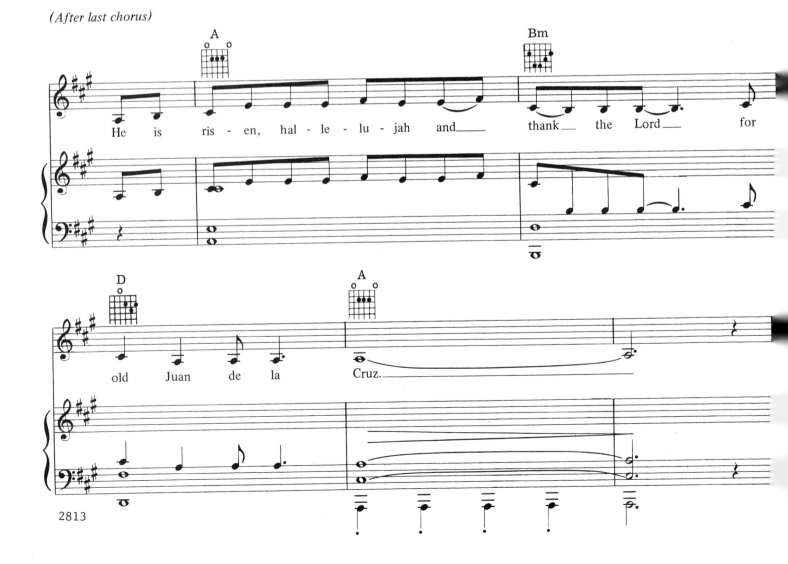

HONEST LULLABY

Words and Music by JOAN BAEZ

KEY: C   CAPO: 5th   PLAY: Am

Moderate 50's Rock

Ear - ly, ear - ly   in   the   game___   I   taught   my - self___   to

2813

330

2813

Last time to Coda

Am / Dm ... D / G ... G / C

I had a moth-er who sang to me___ an hon - est lull-a-

Hon- ey,

D.S. for additional words

by. _____

Yellow, brown and black and white, Our Father bless us all tonight
I bowed my head at the football games, and closed the prayer in Jesus' name
Lusting after football heroes, tough Pachuco little Neroes
Forfeiting my A's for zeroes, futures unforeseen
Spending all my energy in keeping my virginity
And living in a fantasy, in love with Jimmy Dean
If you will be my king, Jimmy Jimmy, I will be your queen
CHORUS
And often have I wondered how the years and I survived
I had a mother who sang to me an honest lullaby

I travelled all around the world, and knew more than the other girls
Of foreign languages and schools, Paris, Rome and Istanbul
But those things never worked for me, the town was much too small, you see
And people have a way of being even smaller yet
But all the same, so life is hard, and no one promised me a garden
Of roses, so I did okay, I took what I could get
And did the things that I might do for those less fortunate

Now, look at you, you must be growing
A quarter of an inch a day
You've already lived near half the years
You'll be when you go away
With your teddy bears and alligators,
Enterprise communicators
All the tiny aviators head into the sky
And while the others play with you,
I hope to find a way with you
And sometimes spend a day with you,
I'll catch you as you fly
Or if I'm worth a mother's salt
I'll wave as you go by.
Repeat Chorus and take Coda

Coda

Am / Dm ... D / G ... C / F

You've got a moth-er who sings___ to you,___ Danc - es on___ the

strings to you___ O - pens her heart___ and brings to you___ an

hon - est lull- a - by.___

FOR SASHA

Written for my German friends who carry the guilt of World War II.

Pg. 335

MICHAEL

"...every folk song that I ever knew once more comes true and love grows old and waxes cold." (From "Sweeter For Me," by Joan Baez.)

Pg. 344

FOR SASHA

Words and Music by JOAN BAEZ

KEY: C CAPO: 5th PLAY: G

pris - on - er of the camps draws nigh. If you are A - bel and

I am Cain ___ for - give me ___ from my bed of pain, . . . I

know not ___ why we die. ___ It was

I who or - dered the build-ing burned, the job was o - ver and

as I turned   a fa - ther__ and his   son

caught   in the flames high a - bove the ground. . .   from cra - dled arms_____   the

boy looked down,. . .   one leap and their lives   were   done. _____   And

2813

MICHAEL

Words and Music by JOAN BAEZ

KEY: C CAPO: 5th PLAY: G

In the time spent in the fog-gy dew
she was Mar - y Ham-il-ton,

with the ra - ven and the dove,
and lov-er of John Ri - ley

and the maid bare-foot she walked the win-ter streets
of con - stant sor - row,

2813

And fill thee up my lov-ing cup fast and to the brim.

How man-y fair and ten-der maids could love as will love as

348

2813

352

fast and to the brim. _____ How

man - y fair and __ ten - der maids _____

_____ will __ ev - er love a -

gain? _____